GAME CHANGER

CHARISSA STASTNY

TANGLED WILLOW
PRESS

TITLES BY CHARISSA STASTNY

Ruled Out Romances

Game Changer

Package Deal

Collateral Hearts

Love Notes

Bending Willow Trilogy

Finding Light

Guarding Secrets

Embracing Mercy

Stand-Alones

Between Hope & the Highway

A Wrinkle in Forever

Of Stone and Sky

Cover Design: Poole Publishing Services

Cover Photo-Game Changer: Tiffany Skelton

ISBN: 978-1-948861-08-3

Game
CHANGER

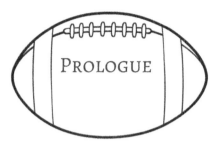

PROLOGUE

I BLAME FALLING in love on orange chicken. No joke. The balance of a human life is so precarious that a simple Chinese dish can throw it all out of whack.

That's what happened to me.

Most life-changing moments stem from mundane and seemingly ordinary decisions. Like the choice to hang out at the student union building with friends, instead of staying home to study. Or the decision of what to buy for lunch, or better yet, what she, a total stranger, chooses to eat. These snap decisions can be just as dramatic as a simple pivot on the field that leads to a game-changing interception.

Love works the same crazy way.

A quiet girl minding her own business, but deciding last minute to order Chinese food, instead of her normal turkey-avocado sandwich, can alter life's path for the most popular football hero on campus.

That's me, by the way—handsome, oblivious hunk, surrounded by beautiful, doting cheerleaders. But I'm getting ahead of myself.

Orange chicken changed my life.

And hers.

With the other insane curve balls life had thrown at me, I never would've guessed the greatest course correction would be caused by a sticky take-out dish carried by a cute, freckled coed. But thank God for small accidents that forced me to look up and notice what was right in front of my eyes.

BLOCKING THE OFFENSE

1

MERIDEE

*O*NCE UPON A time, ice cream cured every sorrow and disappointment. But after working at Ferdinand's for the last three years and scooping thousands of cones to giddy or heartbroken students, not to mention swiping, scrubbing, and scouring creamy stickiness from hidden nooks and crannies, my sweet cure-all had lost its bibbidi-bobbidi-boo power. A case in point could be the dried blackberry ripple I currently chiseled off the stainless-steel counter. If the creamy muck sat long enough inside my stomach, would it cement itself to my intestinal tract as well? I shuddered.

"Hey, Meridee? Can I take my break?"

I glanced up at the new hire, Danny Quick. One of the many wide-eyed, incoming freshmen who'd flooded campus in the last week for orientation. He had yet to live up to his name. I easily scooped five or six cones to his one, and he obsessed over breaks, instead of noticing that counters needed cleaning, tables needed clearing, or floors needed mopping. Danny *Lamenslow* would suit him better.

A cluster of students approaching from the parking lot caught my attention out the window.

"Not yet."

His shoulders slumped. "But I'm beat."

I grabbed a bag of nuts to refill the half-empty canister. How could he be tired when he'd hardly put a dent into his shift? "It's not even seven."

"I had a long night."

"Not my problem." I wiped my hands on my apron. He needed to prioritize and stop partying if he wanted to succeed.

The bells jingled as muscular football players and their female counterparts poured in through the door. Practice must've just ended.

I checked my apron to ensure I didn't have ice cream splattered in awkward places. Not that I cared what the popular jocks and cheer squad thought. I didn't.

"What's good here?" The glass display case trembled as a massive Polynesian, built like a tank, thumped the counter.

"Oh, um..." I stuttered.

Another voice rescued me from my tangled tongue. "Every flavor I've tried is amazing. You can't go wrong, Tiny. Though the huckleberry ripple's my personal kryptonite."

I pulled on a pair of disposable gloves, trying to become invisible as my own personal kryptonite pushed his way up to the front of the line. He focused on tubs of ice cream, giving me time for a quick peek.

His cobalt-blue athletic jersey emphasized muscular arms and made his eyes pop. His dark brown hair appeared damp, as if he'd come straight from the locker room shower. I shivered. This guy—*Barry Tonanhot* I'd nicknamed him—was a Nordic god among men. Both tone and very hot.

He was also completely out of my league.

I braved another peek while he checked out flavors. Usually, he came in alone, and I'd watch from behind the counter and dream. He always opened doors for females, no matter their age or beauty factor, and he left his table clean. No sticky messes. I'd even spotted him picking up trash that wasn't his. Barry Tonanhot's appeal was more than just skin-deep, though his skin was scrumptious. He was a rare breed. A true gentleman. He might be the reason ice cream had lost its magical allure. No flavor could compete with such masculine perfection.

"This place is so...quaint."

Out of the corner of my eye, I noticed Barbie part the crowd like a female Moses. For real. The girl took a step forward, and the rowdy crowd of muscular jocks and dyed blondes stepped back like the Red Sea, allowing her unobstructed passage to Barry Tonanhot, who could go by the name of Ken now that he had Barbie beside him.

I wrinkled my nose. Why did God dish out beauty so unfairly? Wasn't there plenty to pass around to everyone, instead of dumping it all onto those two?

Barbie appeared as though she'd come straight out of her box—flawless makeup, long blond hair, a stylish off-the-shoulder blouse that left none of her curves to the imagination, and the bearing of Aphrodite. I swear, whenever she moved, an invisible slow-motion camera captured her fluidity and grace for everyone to see and worship.

What had she meant by *quaint?* Was she mocking Ferdinand's?

She shouldn't. It was an icon in Pullman. We'd made it onto the top twenty-five college ice cream shops in a recent national poll. With a fifties-diner theme and an area where customers could watch Cougar Gold—our famous cheese—being crafted on the factory floor, Ferdinand's was freaking cool. I'd fallen in love with the place when I'd moved here three years ago for school. I loved working here. My boss was super chill and let me work around my busy schedule.

Bombshell Barbie wrapped herself around Ken, caressing his chiseled jaw.

Why did he have to bring his blasted girlfriend in to ruin the show? He'd been coming in for ice cream almost every week the whole time I'd worked here, and I'd never once seen him with a girl. Which had probably stirred up my useless crush in the first place.

She glanced up at the handwritten menu behind me and pursed her red lips. "Do you have anything that's not loaded with empty calories?"

Was this chick for real? "Uh, this is an ice cream shop, not Whole Foods." Mr. Owens would chide me for my sarcasm, if he were here. As a manager, I needed to be nice to customers, even stupid ones. I took a deep breath. "Would you like a coffee?"

Ken doll chuckled but didn't peek up from his creamy contemplation. He never did. For as many times as he'd come here over the years, he'd never be able to pick me out in a lineup. I remained the faceless girl behind the counter, who scooped his ice cream and collected money that had touched his manly hands. But he'd never really looked at me.

Which was okay. I preferred invisibility over unwanted attention, and Ken garnered lots of that recently.

Even now, I noticed whispering patrons pointing him out to their friends. Maybe he was a star on the field. I wouldn't know. Football ranked right next to cleaning toilets in my book. There was a long list of reasons why I knew Ken and I would never work, besides the fact that he obviously had a girlfriend.

Ken was hot. I was not.

He was social. I was shy.

He was a collegiate athlete. I tripped just thinking about sports.

And now, I could add popularity to the list. I hated attention worse than the hives.

But I wouldn't lose sleep over him—although I might have several steamy dreams with him as the star character, kissing me with those lips, smiling at me with that smile. But it was nothing more than a silly crush on my part. Ken didn't know I existed, which was as it should be.

I had no desire to be close to a guy ever again. In fact, the thought of a guy paying me attention made me choke on my breath. Ken and Barbie could keep their beauty and fame. I preferred my invisibility cloak.

Barbie made a sour face and ordered a raspberry sundae. I turned away to roll my eyes. *No empty calories there, girl.*

Other players called out orders.

I nudged Danny to stop staring and start scooping. "You can take your break after we get through this crowd."

"But that's uh...that's Sticky—"

I tuned out his yammering to hurry to fill orders.

"What are you getting, Sticky Fingers?" A burly guy with facial hair that reminded me of Thor pounded Tonanhot's back, throwing him into the display counter.

Tonanhot shoved the muscular guy in return, even though Thor had him by several inches and at least thirty pounds. That was saying something, since Tonanhot dwarfed most regular guys.

I considered his nickname. Sticky Fingers. Maybe that's what Danny had been trying to spit out before I'd walked away from him. The name sounded as if it belonged to a kid who'd eaten too many s'mores or a juvenile delinquent with a penchant for lifting candy bars from gas stations. Definitely not fitting for a Nordic god.

I filled a plastic cup with soft serve ice cream, wishing someone would call the guy by the name his momma gave him. I knew I'd never talk to him, except to take his order, but I was curious to know his name. My top guesses were Brandt, Tyler, or Luke. Ken could work too, I guess.

"A triple on a waffle cone, but I haven't decided which flavors." Ken's voice matched his looks, smooth and sexy.

"Uh, fudge brownie will only be in stock until the end of the month," I offered, keeping my head down.

His brows pulled together. "No kidding? Then give me a scoop of that. And throw on some huckleberry ripple. That's the best. And..." He wrinkled his nose. It was a perfect nose. No crazy bumps, flaring nostrils, moles, or pointy ends. Just perfection, like everything else about him. "Man, it's so hard to choose."

I stifled a smile. He said that every time. "Maybe the cappuccino chip?" I sucked in my lips, appalled that I'd spoken up again. But I knew for a fact he'd never tried that flavor.

"Ooo. Sounds intriguing. Okay. Make it so, number one."

My lips twitched at his *Star Trek* reference. I focused on making the best triple waffle cone ever, though I doubted he'd notice how carefully I formed each scoop or how much more ice cream I smooshed into his cone than others. But it gave me fodder for bedtime. Tonight, I'd dream of how Ken thanked me for such a spectacular cone before taking my hand and staring into my eyes as he confessed how he couldn't stay away from Ferdinand's because of me. I drew him in each week, not ice cream.

Barbie sidled up against him, making my far-fetched fantasy fizzle out like a dud firecracker.

"Hurry up, Sticky. My ice cream's melting."

Ugh. Sticky was a terrible name for him.

I handed handsome Ken his cone of triple perfection but didn't avert my gaze. With Cheerleader Barbie at his side, he could see no one but her. If I jumped up and down and screamed *Fire!*, I doubted he would flinch.

Ken tossed a ten onto the counter without looking away from his girlfriend. He squeezed her bare shoulders, bringing her into his well-defined chest, where she appeared quite content.

Until she caught me staring.

"Nice hairnet." She gave me a mean-girl smirk.

I ducked my head and opened the cash register to make change. What was she? Five years old? It's not as though I wanted to wear a hairnet, but I'd forgotten an elastic. Would she rather I worked without one and sprinkled a few of my muddy-brown hairs into her sundae? The thought tempted me.

Ken shot me a pity glance I didn't appreciate.

"Here's your change." I threw coins at him.

Barbie tugged her man away from the counter.

I grabbed a rag and squeezed until my fingers ached.

Ken jogged back to the counter and tossed a dollar down. "I think you rock your hairnet." He winked.

My mouth hit the floor. Seriously. No wonder women flocked to him. I had no idea what he did on the field, but who cared. With that smile and those gorgeous blue eyes, he could get whatever he wanted.

"Thanks for this." He held up his waffle cone. "It's perfect."

Before I could respond—assuming I could've formed words—he returned to Barbie, who was glaring bullets at me.

The stunning couple found a table, and a crowd accosted them. Papers and napkins were thrust out for him to sign. Barry Tonanhot threw out that smile to any and all, making me realize the one he'd given me was nothing special. Just him on auto-pilot.

When no other customers appeared, I told Danny to take his break. His lame and slow movements turned quick and peppy as he high-tailed it through the swinging door to the break room.

I began a furious wipe-down of the stainless-steel counters as a few more customers entered. I filled orders, while ignoring the rowdy jocks and cheerleaders around the shop. When the popular people began filtering out, tossing cups, spoons, and napkins into the trash bins, Barbie glided back to her table. Maybe she'd forgotten her purse. Her platinum-blond hair probably didn't hide a brilliant mind.

"Hey, Hairnet!" she yelled from across the room.

I turned to find her smirking at me. *Me?* I mouthed, touching my neck.

"Yeah, you. There's a spill over here you need to clean up." She snapped her fingers. "Pronto."

I wish I could say she cackled as she flew out on her broom, but sadly, she had a melodic giggle that probably made Ken smile even bigger, if that was possible.

So not fair.

The door closed behind her, and I released a weary sigh and headed to the corner to check out the mess. I came to an abrupt halt at her vacated table. In raspberry syrup, someone—a certain perfect-looking someone, I'm sure—had drawn an awful stick figure with what had to be a hairnet warping her hair.

I shook my head and began scrubbing at her juvenile artwork.

I'd never liked Barbies, even as a little girl.

2

PARKER

STRETCHING MY STIFF fingers, I sank into a lounger on the first floor of the Compton Union Building, or CUB, as it was commonly referred to among students, and reached for my lukewarm hamburger.

Fame sucked at times.

Don't get me wrong. I enjoyed attention as much as the next guy, but I missed a few things from the old days—like two weeks ago old, when I'd been a second-stringer with no hope of actually playing in a game. Back when I'd warmed the bench while Walton had lit up the field, but at least I could grab lunch and eat it still hot because nobody recognized me and wanted my autograph.

Those days were over.

In our first home game last week, I'd become a rising star due to Walton's career-ending accident, a few incredible catches, and pure dumb luck that some YouTuber had put it all to video with a catchy tune and nickname for me. That video had gone viral, and ESPN sportscasters were even talking about me. Now, I couldn't use the john without someone calling me by my media moniker—Sticky Fingers. I feared my sticky fingers might develop carpal tunnel from signing so many shirts, hats, balls, and notebooks. One girl had even made me sign her thong. Talk about awkward.

Tiny Mo nudged me, knocking me halfway out of my seat.

"Watch it, little guy." I moved my drink out of the way of his massive arm.

He tilted his chin in the direction of Bookie's checkout line. "There's your woman."

I glanced over my shoulder and felt my pulse quicken as Lily Meyers glided across the open seating area. Each table and couch she passed had a domino effect. Guys' heads tipped as they watched her graceful journey, wishing she was in their arms or laps. I knew this because my head and gaze did the same. Lily was impossible to ignore. The only difference between me and the other chumps was she actually locked eyes with me and threw me a promising smile.

I sat up straighter and licked my lips. Despite what Tiny had said, she wasn't my woman. Yet. But she'd been my dream for the past two years. Last year, I'd watched from the bench as she'd cheered for our team—and especially Tim Avery, the all-star quarterback who she'd been dating at the time—and had mourned the fact that she didn't notice me.

But she saw me now.

One benefit of my newfound fame.

I stood and puffed out my chest as she approached with her entourage of cheerleader friends.

"Hey, Sticky Fingers." If she'd been a car thief, she would've had me hot-wired and my engine revved with that simple greeting.

"Hey, gorgeous." I grinned, proud that I hadn't stuttered.

She pulled me down onto the olive-green couch and crushed up against me. My heart rate increased. Having devoted most of my time to football during high school and college and working full-time when I wasn't practicing, I hadn't had much chance to mingle with goddesses of Lily's caliber. They'd required way more time than I'd had to give.

Her hand slid up my thigh, making me want to roll over and wag my tail. But I held it together. Despite my lack of experience, I wasn't stupid. I knew a girl like Lily would tire of a guy who acted too whipped. If I wanted to score a touchdown and have a lasting relationship, not just catch a pass or two before she grew tired and moved on, I needed to play a little hard to get. But not too much. I didn't want to lose her, either.

"You ready for the game tomorrow, Sticky?"

"I was born ready." From watching the other starters, I knew confidence was key, though the thought of tomorrow's game made me want to puke. "What about you? Are you ready to cheer me on from the sidelines in your sexy spandex?"

She moved her hand further up my leg, making it difficult to breathe. "I'm ready to do a lot more than that, baby."

Her innuendo didn't fly over my head. I wasn't clueless. And she wasn't being too subtle. I took a bite of my burger. Lily was a flirt. She'd been serious last year when she'd been engaged to Tim Avery, but after he'd been sacked in the second to last game of the season and had busted his knee and all his chances for the NFL, she'd dumped him. At least, that's what the guys claimed. More likely, she'd seen Avery for the putz he really was and had ended things because of that. But still, I needed to play it cool.

I wanted more than a fling. I wanted forever.

I chewed my burger but choked when Lily's frisky hand surprised me under the table. The guys guffawed as I pounded my chest and coughed. This woman was trying to kill me.

"You trying to swallow that burger whole, Sticky?" Carsen swatted my back hard enough to send pieces of burger flying from my mouth.

The girls squealed. "Gross!"

Lily winked. The big tease.

Carsen flicked the side of my head and tossed a football to Jacob, our quarterback. "Throw us some balls, Jake?" He smirked. "Best of five, Sticky. Loser buys drinks tonight after practice.

"I'm eating." I focused on my burger. Not that I thought I would lose, but I didn't have any cash to pay for drinks if I did.

"Afraid I'll show you up in front of everyone?"

I glared at him. Carsen had been riding me ever since Lily had stopped flirting with him to tease me. He made everything into a contest between us and tried to make me look bad every chance he got. I was sick of his attitude.

I pounded my hands together and stood. "Not at all. Just don't want to make you look like a fool."

His sneer said it was game on.

Jacob palmed the football as Carsen strutted across the CUB like a junkyard pit bull. I took another bite of burger before jogging over to take up a position next to him. The chatter of the lunch crowd increased as students focused on us.

Lily blew me a kiss.

I winked at her.

Unfortunately, Jacob chose that moment to launch the ball. Carsen outmaneuvered me and made the first catch.

"In your face, Sticky." He paraded around like an alpha dog for our clapping audience.

17

I glared at Jacob. He'd thrown it early on purpose to give his friend the advantage.

"You'll get it this time, Sticky Fingers," Lily called.

My determination to annihilate Carsen skyrocketed. I watched McGuen, cluing in to the slight tilt of his shoulder, and took off to the right before the ball even left his hand. I scrambled over a couch to reach over Carsen's outstretched hands to snap the pigskin from the air in front of him.

He shoved me. "Cheater."

"I caught that fair and square, dude."

When I caught the next two passes as well, Carsen began stomping around and accusing Jacob of throwing to my side. What a tool. Our tight end had speed—his nickname was Swift—but I could predict Jacob's intentions with almost uncanny precision. That gave me a slight edge over Carsen.

I waved the ball under his nose. "Three for four, my man." Normally, I wouldn't rub my luck in his face. But he deserved it.

"Best of seven," he yelled to Jacob. He raised a challenging brow, daring me to argue.

I shrugged, resisting the urge to make the loser sign with my fingers.

Lily blew kisses, making me hungry for some real ones. Forget my burger. I pretended to catch her token from the air, but still observed Jacob out of the corner of my eye. As he pulled back his arm, I discerned a faint shift of his weight to the rear and knew he'd throw long. Before the ball released, I darted behind Carsen. He tugged at my shirt, but I used my left hand to free myself and weaved between tables and couches. The ball sailed over my head, and I launched myself into the air to grab it. The ball grazed my fingertips, but before I could tuck it into my chest, all forward momentum came to a jarring halt.

A girl screamed and I crashed to the ground midst food, styrofoam, and a petite coed who'd been holding it all on a tray.

I rubbed my head and blinked as the girl I'd just tackled sputtered and looked around with a dazed expression. Orange chicken and sauce dripped from her hair and cream-colored blouse. Soda-soaked rice stuck to her arms and cheeks. My head still spun, but luckily, I'd remained mostly unscathed.

Laughter erupted behind me. I peeked over my shoulder to see my friends slapping backs and holding stomachs at my predicament. Especially Carsen. I rolled my eyes, before turning to face my victim.

She winced as she surveyed spilled soda and more orange chicken than should be legal for a girl her size to order.

"Are you okay?" I groaned and rolled to my knees. Tile wasn't as forgiving as turf.

"Yeah." She leaned over to scoop rice and sticky chicken onto her tray.

"Here. Let me get that. I'm the one who—"

Carsen pounded my back, knocking me into her. The girl flinched and hugged herself.

"Good tackle, Harrington. Maybe Coach should put you on the line with Tiny Mo."

"Bite me," I snapped.

The girl's brown eyes glistened with tears, making me feel horrible.

"I'm sorry," I said again. What had I been thinking jumping like that in this crowded venue?

"Nice form, Sticky." Lily approached.

My victim lowered her head and shoveled the orange disaster onto her tray as though it was food in a famine. I used my hands to sweep soda-soaked rice toward the tray she held perpendicular to the floor.

"Ew." Lily tugged on my bicep. "Let her clean up her own mess."

"Grab some napkins, will you?" I said.

She huffed and marched over to Carsen.

I shook my head. "Here." I dumped a peace offering onto the girl's tray.

"Can you just leave?" Her pretty eyes flashed. "People are staring."

It surprised me that she hadn't melted into a giddy puddle when I'd flashed my pearly whites. Most girls did. Of course, I'd never run into a girl and dressed her in orange chicken.

"I really am sorry. I didn't see you."

"Yeah, that's obvious."

Cute freckles sprinkled her cheeks and nose. A few dotted her forehead.

"You have sauce right here." I touched the side of my nose.

She swiped a finger across the wrong side.

"You missed."

"Will you just go?"

A janitor approached with a cart. "Ay, ay, ay. What happened here?" He leaned over to touch my orange-splattered victim's shoulder as she struggled to single-handedly make the mess disappear. "Don't worry about it, sweetheart. I'll clean it up. That's why they pay me the big bucks."

She turned her golden gaze on him, making me smirk. I bet she got anything she wanted out of guys with that *woe-is-me* act.

"I'm so sorry."

My eyes bulged. If Lily or any of the other cheerleaders had been in her shoes, they'd be throwing a hissy fit, not apologizing. I thought all girls were that way.

"It's my fault," I said.

The janitor lit up like the Fourth of July as he recognized me. "Sticky Fingers! You ready for the big game tomorrow?"

I wondered if the girl recognized me now.

Carsen butted into the conversation. "He'd better be."

The janitor started sweeping. "Sticky Fingers *and* Swift. Today's my lucky day. Do you guys think you could sign my shirt?"

Miss Orange Chicken fumbled with her backpack and pushed into the gathering crowd. As she disappeared into a sea of students, I blinked.

Maybe she hadn't recognized me.

I elbowed Carsen's side. "I'll be right back, man." I pushed through the throng of gawkers to catch up to my victim at a restroom.

"Hey, wait."

She jumped and turned to face me.

"You left before I could make that up to you." I wiped my fingers against my jeans.

"Don't worry about me. You've done your duty, Sticky Fingers." Her tone sounded mocking, not adoring. "Best return to your fans." She pushed inside the ladies' room, clearly showing she wasn't one of them.

The door started to swing closed, and I leaped forward, stepping into no-man's land. "Let me at least pay for your lunch and shirt." I pulled out my wallet and winced. Only three lousy bucks. "This is all I have on me." I held the bills out. "But if you give me your Venmo name, I can send more." I tried not to stare at the revealing stain on her blouse that had my mind going places it shouldn't. She had very nice curves.

Her eyes widened as she focused beyond me.

I turned to see that my groupies had followed and were almost upon us.

"Just go." She fled into a stall, slamming the door behind her, leaving me looking like a perv in the women's restroom.

I hurried into the hallway just as the crowd of autograph-seekers swarmed me. Blowing out a deep breath, I retrieved a Sharpie from my pocket. With one last look at the closed restroom door, I shook my head and started signing a football program.

I'd tried to make amends and be a gentleman, as my mama had taught me. It wasn't my fault Miss Orange Chicken had refused my efforts.

So why did I feel so bad?

3

MERIDEE

INKLING BELLS MADE my jaw tick. I didn't mind my job. In fact, I loved it most days. But if I could change one detail, I'd eliminate the annoying bells that announced each new customer. Whenever they jingled, I wanted to throw a rag at the door. There'd been non-stop customers today, so the bells rang in my head even when they didn't chime in real-time. It didn't help my mood, since I'd come straight here from pulling a twelve-hour shift at the hospital. I was functioning on pure adrenaline. Working as a nursing assistant one day a week, on top of my hours at Ferdinand's and juggling a full load of college classes, might not have been the wisest course of action. But I needed to keep my certification current. Hospital time would count toward work hours required by PA programs down the road.

Who needed sleep?

I hissed under my breath as five massive football players and the same number of gorgeous girls shoved into the end of the line, Bombshell Barbie and Tackling Ken among them.

Barbie draped herself on Ken's arm and tickled his chin. "I don't know why you like this place, Sticky." The woman used the worst endearments. "There's always a line out the door and nowhere to sit."

"Because it's the best ice cream in the city," Ken said. "Possibly the state."

Mr. Owens, my boss, should use the guy for publicity. Not only was he eye-candy, but he spoke sweet words as well.

21

Ken wrapped his arms around Barbie's waist and whispered sweet-nothings in her ear. At least, that's what I assumed since she giggled.

I handed a Tin Lizzy classic to a customer. "Anything else?" No sense focusing on the Mattel dolls being gross. I had a huge line to please before I could rest my aching wrists.

I helped two more people before my gaze was drawn to the perfect couple again. Though I despised seeing them together, I couldn't resist stealing peeks at the man who played a major role in my dreams each night.

Barbie stepped up to the counter and Bryce attended to her. Luckily, with the crowd, she hadn't spotted me yet. Her Nordic god dropped his hands from her waist to track bins of ice cream.

"What can I get you?" I asked the huge Polynesian next in line.

I heard Barbie order a cherry Italian soda as I kept my head tucked and scooped a triple for the tattooed islander.

The Thor look-alike waved Barbie over to the side, where customers could watch Cougar Gold being made behind giant windows in the adjoining alcove. She glanced at Ken, who looked between apple cup crisp and caramel cashew, before she grabbed her fancy soda and bee-lined it over to Thor.

My eyes widened when the jock pinched her tush. What the hay?

I turned to gauge Ken's reaction, but he had his head bowed, still pondering the combination of flavors for his triple. He hadn't seen a thing. I whipped my focus back to Barbie, who giggled as Thor leaned down to kiss her before pulling her out of view.

Holy Brahma Bull.

Did Ken know his girlfriend was playing him?

Bryce and I whittled the line down to only two fan girls, who fawned over Barbie's cheated-on Ken doll as he concentrated on the tubs of ice cream behind the glass. I motioned for Bryce to take his ten as Danny helped the giddy girls.

I stood there, waiting for Ken to make up his mind and order without looking up. Heaven forbid, he recognize me. Not that he would. But just in case, I stared at the counter.

"Hmm, let's see." His head stayed bowed. "I'll have a triple waffle cone with a scoop of caramel cashew and..." He scratched his head, as though solving a physics problem. "...a scoop of huckleberry ripple, and I guess I'll try a scoop of that..."

He paused.

I peeked up to see if he was pointing at a flavor. No such luck. He was staring at me.

"Y-you," he sputtered.

I cringed, wishing a sinkhole would open up in the floor and swallow me.

"You're the girl I crashed into in the CUB two days ago, aren't you?"

My cheeks burned and my throat scratched like sandpaper. "W-what was the last flavor you wanted?" He hadn't finished ordering.

"Oh, yeah." His gaze dropped but shot right back up to stare at me again.

"Your last flavor?" I determined to keep him on task.

His brows furrowed. "I guess I'll have the licorice, since it's new."

I attempted to ignore the sexy man gaping at me as though I'd sprouted horns. The tightening in my chest and labored breathing proved my efforts vain.

Where was Barbie when I needed her?

Oh, right. She and Thor had disappeared together. Hopefully, no children ran into the hallway to observe machines making cheese. They'd receive more than curds and whey education if they did.

I held out Ken's cone, staring at the space beyond his shoulder. "Who's paying for all this?" No one had paid yet from his group.

The guy who'd been putting moves on Barbie a minute ago swaggered into view and slugged Ken's shoulder. "He is."

Considering how Ken's lips tightened, I doubted that had been his plan.

"It's on Sticky Fingers," Thor, stealer-of-girlfriends, shouted.

The popular girls and muscular guys in the room cheered.

Ken scowled. "Guess I'm paying."

"How noble of you." With friends like his, who needed enemies?

A dimple dented his cheek as he grinned.

So unfair. Like he didn't already have a surplus of sexy, he also had a dimple? How had I not noticed that before?

I announced his grand total, and he dug in his wallet to pay. Then Ken lifted his cone and leaned forward so I had no other choice but to look at him, since he'd encroached into my space.

"Thanks for this," he said. "It's perfect. As usual." He sauntered over to join his rowdy, two-timing friends, leaving me speechless.

4

PARKER

*W*EAVING THROUGH RED tables, I headed over to join Lily after paying for everyone's orders. Stupid Carsen, sticking me with the bill. He was just sore because Lily had chosen me, not him. We'd made it official last night, after the game. Thankfully, I had been on fire again, and so had McGuen. We'd worked well together, proving I wasn't just a one-time wonder. Lily had been my biggest fan, even hanging out with me afterward while McGuen and I were interviewed. A heady experience.

"There's my man," Lily purred as I joined her.

I rested my hand on her knee and licked my cone. "Bleak!" I spit the gray nastiness into a napkin. Seeing the ice cream scooper, and realizing she was the same girl I'd crashed into the other day, had flustered me, making me order the first flavor in view. A huge mistake.

I snatched Lily's discarded plastic top from her soda and nudged the scoop of disgusting muck into it. "Sorry."

She giggled. "I take it you don't like that flavor."

I yanked another napkin from the metal receptacle to wipe my tongue. "That's one I'll only recommend to my enemies. Maybe Carsen." I sank my teeth into the next scoop. Huckleberry ripple. "But this one is worthy of the gods. And goddesses. Want a bite?" I held my cone out to her.

"You're adorable." She took a dainty lick and ran her fingers through my hair. "You should come over to my place tonight." Her husky voice made my heart pound, aching for what she insinuated. But it was too soon. I hadn't even taken her on a real date yet.

"I have to study."

"You could study anatomy with me." She winked.

A goofy grin plastered my face. "Tempting." I glanced over at the freckled worker behind the counter to curb my wicked impulse. She had no idea how much I wanted her, especially when she teased me like this. But I'd promised Mom when I'd left home that I'd be a gentleman and not have sex without serious commitment.

I still couldn't believe the ice cream girl was the same girl I'd run over in the CUB. No wonder she hadn't appeared happy to see me. After covering her in orange chicken and possibly bruising her backside, I'd tried to give her three bucks and call it good. Lame. Now, I realized that I'd seen her before our crash. I'd been seeing her regularly for two years at this decadent dessert Mecca. She made way bigger cones than her coworkers, so I always strategically placed myself in line and let others go ahead to ensure she took my order and no one else.

With her focus on a customer, I tried to determine the color of her hair. Reddish brown. Maybe dark strawberry blond. It was unique, whatever you called it. She wore a ponytail today, so I didn't have to worry about Lily teasing her about a hairnet. I tried to recall what her hair had looked like all down when I'd crashed into her but kept drawing a blank. Of course, her hair had been covered in orange sauce and soda. Probably not the most flattering style on anyone. The girl was adorable. Not stunning, like Lily, but cute. She was shorter than Lily by a few inches. Yesterday, in the orange chicken-covered blouse she'd been wearing, I'd noticed tempting curves. Today, her ice cream splattered t-shirt and apron hid those.

Lily blew in my ear. I closed my eyes, still on a cloud that she was my girl now. Life was looking up.

Bells rang. I glanced up and spotted Riley, my buddy from my *nobody* days. "Hey, Ry." I waved.

My quiet friend returned my wave and headed to the front. He still sat the bench, though he was a senior like me. It'd done a number on his confidence. Maybe hanging out with cool people would give him the boost he needed. That's why I'd invited him.

Lily placed her hand against my thigh and leaned over to claim my lips. And not just a peck. Like last night, after I'd asked her to be my girl, she practically attacked me. Not that I was complaining. Her moist mouth opened and her tongue teased. I set my mostly eaten cone on a napkin and wrapped my arms around her. I didn't really care for PDA, but who was I to turn down a goddess?

"Get a room," Carsen called from a nearby table.

I pulled away, cheeks prickling with heat as the guys wolf-whistled. I checked where Riley was and retrieved my melting cone.

My friend stood at the cash register, flirting with the cute worker. She smiled as she handed him his change, and wow! That smile transformed her. She'd definitely never smiled at me that way. Of course, I'd never given her a reason. That reminded me—I owed her money to cover her meal and a new shirt. Orange chicken couldn't have come out of that gauzy material easily, if at all.

I swiped a napkin across my mouth and stood as Riley approached. "Hey, man. Glad you could make it. Keep Lily company for a sec, will ya? I'll be right back." I jogged to the counter to make things right with my crash victim.

She had her back to me, washing the counter.

"Psst," I hissed to get her attention.

The girl faced me, her thick-lashed, bottomless brown eyes brimming with emotion. Again, I had the thought that she probably got whatever she wanted from guys. She had the whole damsel-in-distress look down.

"Here." I held out a twenty. It was all I had left after paying for ten orders. "I feel awful about what happened the other day."

"I don't want your money." She pushed my hand aside as Lily sidled up next to me.

"What are you doing, Sticky?" She latched onto my arm.

"Oh, uh," I stammered, "the worker here made a mistake tallying up our order. I didn't want to shortchange her. Go wait at the table, babe. I'll join you in a sec."

Lily didn't move, so I threw the money onto the counter. "Please take it," I whispered, leaning forward to catch the worker's attention. She never seemed to look at me.

Lily patted my cheek. "You're so sweet, Sticky buns."

I frowned at her dumb nickname.

She faced the ice cream girl. "I agree with my boyfriend. Keep the money, honey." She leaned forward to whisper, but I still heard her. "Just promise to buy concealer to cover those freckles. They do nothing for you."

I watched the sting of her insult make impact and turn the cute work-er's face beet red. I wanted to say something to make her smile again. Her freckles weren't ugly. I liked them.

But Lily tugged me away. "Have a nice day."

I followed her outside to my old pickup, feeling like a jerk for not speaking up. "Why did you say that to her?" I said as I opened her door.

"What?" Lily appeared as innocent as a lamb.

"About her freckles. They weren't bad."

She climbed into the cab of my truck. "They weren't good, either. Obviously, no one's given her beauty tips. Trust me, I did her a favor." She caressed my jaw.

"I think you embarrassed her."

Lily cocked her head. "You really are a sweetheart, Sticky. But stop worrying. Truth sometimes hurts, but she'll thank me later." She wrinkled her nose. "Speaking of truth, you need to buy a new set of wheels. This thing's a heap of junk."

I ran a hand along the frame of my truck, counting to ten before I spoke. "I'll never get rid of my girl. Meryl and I have been through a lot together."

"Like what? Cancer?" She giggled.

I shut her door and walked around to my side. Girls could be annoying, even perfect ones like Lily. All they cared about were material things like fancy cars and expensive restaurants. Yes, Meryl was old, but she was reliable. And paid for.

I climbed in and put the truck in reverse. As I pulled away, Riley walked out of Ferdinand's, head bowed. "Shoot!" I smacked the steering wheel. "I forgot about Ry." Not only had I not stood up for the freckled worker, but I'd ditched my friend to boot.

"Him?" Lily pushed hair over her shoulder. "He's easily forgettable." She slid closer on the bench seat to nibble my neck. "You're going places now, baby. You don't need guys like him holding you down. You have me."

Her hand slid up my leg, and I wondered how she could arouse and annoy me at the same time. Was this normal? I hadn't been serious with anyone since high school. I'd dated, but no one had intrigued me as Lily had.

"He's my friend."

"You have new friends now." She blew in my ear again. It was fast becoming my new favorite thing. And she was right. I'd long craved the acceptance of Lily's group. They were tight, like family. They threw cool parties. And they liked me. I wasn't overlooked anymore. If roles were reversed, I wouldn't hold Riley back from hanging with the cool crowd. I'd encourage him. Besides, I'd still see him at practices and stuff. We might not hang out as much as we used to, but nobody could have it all. Sacrifices had to be made if I wanted to keep my dream girl happy.

5

MERIDEE

ARBIE LED KEN outside, and I crumpled the twenty-dollar bill in my hand and stormed into the back, bumping into Bryce as he exited the break room.

"Whoa. Are you okay?" He steadied me.

"I'm fine. Get back to work. It's busy up front."

His brows furrowed. "I just—"

"I'm taking a break and don't want to be interrupted. Understand?"

He held up his hands as if to ward off a crazy lady and made his escape.

I kicked a stool over and growled. How could Ken have embarrassed me like that, calling the attention of his stunning Rottweiler girlfriend to lash out at me? I'd imagined him better than that. Better than *her*.

I'd never asked him to pay for my meal or ruined blouse, yet he believed he could dish out pity and I'd lap it up like one of his groupies.

I stamped my foot. He'd been much more fun to hero-worship before he'd become popular and got a girlfriend.

The crumpled twenty looked sad in my hand. When Ken returned, which the ice cream addict would, I'd throw the bill back at him and tell him where to stuff it.

Barbie's words echoed in my head. *I agree with my boyfriend. Boyfriend. Boyfriend.*

I hated how sweet the venomous she-devil sounded on my damaged eight-track memory loop.

Keep the money, honey. Honey. Honey. I pounded my fists together and marched over to the mirror hanging behind the door.

Just promise to buy concealer to cover those freckles. Freckles. Freckles.

I touched my cheek. Though I hated to admit it, she had a point. I'd let myself go after Brody, in an effort to be invisible. But I'd never intended to be ugly. Homely people stood out as much or more than beautiful ones. I'd just wanted to be somewhere in the middle. Overlooked.

Danny peeked in at me. "There's a customer who—"

"I told Bryce I didn't want to be interrupted."

"B-but he wants—"

"Danny, handle it yourself. You've worked here for three weeks. I don't bug you on your breaks, so stop hounding me on mine."

His shoulders sagged. "But he—"

"Give him a free ice cream and send him on his way." Did I need to spell out everything for the freshman?

"That's not what he wants," he grumbled, but the door closed.

I opened my locker and stuffed the dratted twenty into my purse. Then I took it out again. Better to carry the blasted thing in my apron pocket until the irritating culprit returned, so I could show him what I thought of his pity offering.

I stepped in front of the mirror again.

Stupid freckles! They'd been the bane of my existence since junior high. Maybe I should cover them up—not for Barbie's sake, but because I didn't want anyone else to notice them.

But I refused to use Ken's precious money.

I could buy my own dang foundation, thank you very much.

6

PARKER

*T*HE DUCT WORK and ceiling vents in the weight room stared down at me as I hefted fifty pound weights above my chest and bared my teeth. Darren acted as my spotter. Coach had made me increase my weight circuit to an hour, and I was feeling the strain. Big time.

Darren counted to twenty, and I let the dumbbells fall behind me.

"Take a breather," he said.

Gladly. My muscles screamed. A sheen of sweat plastered my skin. I leaned over to gulp air. Despite the pain, I loved pushing my body to the edge of exhaustion. Almost made me forget about the Ferdinand's incident two days ago, when Lily had pointed out the cute worker's freckles and embarrassed her. I still felt horrible for that.

I rubbed my nose. Not that I blamed Lily. She'd felt she was helping the girl and hadn't grasped how hurtful her words had come across. I just wished I hadn't stood mute and let her lead me out of the shop like a lapdog. I should've found a way to assure the worker that her freckles were fine. Refreshing even.

Of course, that might not have gone over well with my girlfriend.

"Okay." I panted. "I'm ready."

I started my next weight circuit, half-listening to Darren boast about his latest conquest. When I finished, I laid on the floor and groaned.

"Good job, man." He high-fived me on the floor. "You sure you don't want to join us tonight?"

I shook my head. "I have homework."

"Lily won't be happy."

I made a face. Keeping my girl happy was harder than I'd expected it to be. But I had to keep up my grades.

Darren took off to join Jacob and the others at a bar across town. I rubbed my aching knees and stood. When the dizziness passed, I trudged to the showers and rinsed off before icing my shoulders. I dressed, then chugged down a protein drink and headed to my truck.

But my mind wouldn't stop nagging.

Mom had raised me to be kind to others, not tear them down. And as well-meaning as Lily had intended to be, I knew in my gut that she'd humiliated the shy worker.

I had to make things right somehow.

My stomach churned as I drove to the end of Stadium Road. What if the girl didn't want to talk to me? I'd been a coward, not saying anything to void Lily's stinging remark. That was just as bad as if I'd said the words.

I parked and tugged at my collar. Maybe I'd test the waters. Order ice cream as usual. If the girl acted upset, I'd apologize. If she acted chill, I'd know I'd blown Lily's remark into something bigger than it really was and could forget the incident.

I spotted a tall blonde flipping the *Open* sign to *Closed*.

Crap! Time had gotten away from me.

I sprinted up the steps and banged on the door, making the poor worker jump out of her boots. Smashing my face into the glass, I pointed to my watch.

"I have two minutes. Let me in, please."

The blond worker laughed and unlocked the door.

"Thank you." I stomped my feet as I entered. "Can I get a huckleberry ice cream?"

She giggled. "You're Parker Harrington on the football team, right?"

I bowed. "The one and only."

She led me to the empty counter. I glanced around, but didn't see the short, freckled worker.

"My manager might not want me doing this," she whispered, "but there's a quarter bin of huckleberry I'm supposed to toss. I could let you take it."

"You're an angel."

She giggled again.

The door to the back swung open, and the cutie I'd come to see stepped in with her back to us, lugging a crate across the black and white tiles.

"Tara," she said, "can you grab the mop and take it back to the freezer? I knocked over a carton of cream."

The giggling blonde—Tara, I assumed—gave me an apologetic look. *Sorry,* she mouthed as she grabbed a mop and disappeared.

I watched the petite manager struggle with the load that was far too heavy for her. "Here. Let me carry that for you," I offered.

At the sound of my voice, she screamed and fell onto her backside.

I reached down to help her up.

She batted my hand away. "What are you doing here?" She scrambled to her feet and brushed off her pants. "Tara!" she shouted, "I thought I told you to lock up."

Tara peeked out at us. "I was—"

"I beat her inside." I winked at Tara. "Figured I could buy an ice cream since I was here."

The cute manager scowled. Thick foundation that didn't quite match her skin tone hid her freckles. Looked like she'd taken Lily's comment to heart. "Well, you figured wrong. We're closed." She tried to shoo me out the door.

I lifted the heavy crate. "Where do you need this?"

"I don't need your help." She straightened her shoulders and shoved her hand in her pocket. "And I don't need your pity either."

She tried to hand me a crinkled twenty but I shook my head. "That wasn't pity. It was me being a gentleman. I owe you a new shirt."

"Just take your money and leave." She tried to toss the twenty into the crate but it fell to the floor.

Tara joined us, mop in hand. "Meridee, I told him he could take the bin of huckleberry since you said we couldn't sell it after today."

Her name was Meridee. I tucked that piece of information away as I set the crate on the floor between us.

She placed her hands on her hips. "Tara had no right to do that. I'm the manager and I say it's going in the dumpster. Now take your twenty and go." She picked up the bill and threw it at me again.

I smiled. She kind of reminded me of a ticked-off Tinkerbell. Small, cute, and feisty. I held out a hand. "I'm Parker. Nice to meet you, Meridee."

Her cheeks colored, but she made no attempt to shake my hand. "Y-you need to leave, Parker, or I'll...I'll call the campus police."

I laughed. She was super cute when she was flustered. "Ah, now that'd make their day. Can you imagine the headline?" I waved my hand. "Star

33

football player arrested for stealing expired huckleberry ice cream from campus creamery." I winked. "Might be good publicity for both of us."

Meridee frowned.

"Let's compromise. I'll help you move this crate to wherever it needs to go, and you let Tara give me the huckleberry ice cream. We both win. You don't break your back, and Tara doesn't break her promise to me."

Once more, the girl bent to pick up the twenty and surprised me by pressing close. She slid the bill into the front pocket of my jeans, making me hyper-aware of her dainty body with the killer curves.

She stepped away. "Now, out." She pointed to the door.

I cleared my throat, breathless from the way her hand had almost burned through my denim pocket. What the freak? I had a girlfriend. No way should I be having the hots for someone else. And I didn't. I was just missing Lily since I couldn't hang out with her tonight. And I felt bad for this girl. That's all.

A loud crash came from the back room.

"Don't worry. It's just me." A middle-aged man with a comb-over entered, stopping short when he spotted me. Meridee opened her mouth to speak, but he beat her to it. "Parker Harrington? Sticky Fingers? Is it really you?"

I grinned. "Last I checked."

Meridee stiffened as the man bounced on his feet. "Wow! This is such an honor. My son thinks you're the bomb.com. He'll be upset he missed you." He turned to Meridee. "Do you know who this is?"

"Yes." She tapped her foot. "His name is Sticky Fingers and he was just leaving." She grabbed my arm and gestured to the door. "Weren't you?"

Once again, my skin tingled beneath her fingertips. "Uh..." I stepped away from her, "...as soon as I get my ice cream."

Meridee tried to act professional, but I could tell under that layer of calm she wanted to wring my neck. I stifled a smile. It actually felt refreshing to be treated so normally. Maybe that's all this was between us. She didn't care one bit about my celebrity status. In fact, it seemed to annoy her.

"Mr. Owens, Tara was locking up and this *gentleman*," she frowned at me, "pushed his way in and demanded we give him the rest of the huckleberry ice cream. But it's expired. By law we must throw it out or we could get fined by the health department. If he took it, he could get sick and die. What would the poor team do then without its sticky fingers?"

I chuckled at her dramatic report. "It wasn't quite like that," I said to the older man. "You see, Tara offered it to me instead of throwing it out. And I have a stomach of steel. Don't worry about me getting sick. Flu bugs and vomit-inducing bacteria flee at the sight of this body." I flexed both biceps and growled, making Tara squeal and Mr. Owens clap. Meridee looked like she wanted to smack me.

I pulled out my wallet. "Of course, I'd be willing to pay."

Mr. Owens shook his head. "Mercy no. I'd never dream of charging you for expired inventory. Take the ice cream as a token of my heartfelt appreciation for a job well done. Go, Cougs!" He punched the air. "Do you want any other flavors?"

"That's mighty kind of you." I winked at Meridee. "But I'm afraid I'll be hard up to find room in my freezer for this one. But let me pay. I don't want to skim off Ferdinand's. This place is my favorite."

"I insist." Mr. Owens marched past a pouting Meridee to retrieve the bin of ice cream from behind the counter. "Here you go, Sticky Fingers." He presented the huge tub to me. "Come back for more when you're ready. It'll be on the house."

"Thank you, sir. Do you mind if I move that crate before I leave? I told Meridee I'd move it for her if she let me take the ice cream." I waggled my brows as she scowled. "Don't want to renege on my promise."

She yanked the mop from Tara's hand and did an about-face, disappearing through the swinging door without a second glance at me.

The crinkled twenty-dollar bill cut into my hand, making me growl.

The stubborn woman had won our battle again.

⑦
MERIDEE

*W*HY WERE MEN such idiots? I scrubbed caramel off the counter, wishing it was as easy to scrape a certain man from my mind. Parker Harrington had ticked me off last night when he'd barged into the shop after closing to make a nuisance of himself. It was one thing for him to shove his way into my dreams, but he needed to stay away from me in real life. Guys like him were bad for my health. Part of me hoped he'd gotten sick from eating expired ice cream. But my luck, he'd be rushed to the hospital and I'd have to empty his bedpan on my one night on duty.

His ego was the size of Texas, which is where he must come from, judging by his cowboy drawl. I couldn't believe he still thought he could buy me with that twenty. But I'd showed him I wasn't one of his silly fans that could be charmed by his grin and a Jackson waved in front of my face.

I pounded my rag against the counter, earning an eyebrow raise from Bryce.

"Sorry." I forced a smile. Mr. Owens had taken me aside after the Parker fiasco to say I needed to be friendlier. He'd said I came across as intimidating to my coworkers. "This stain's stubborn."

Derp. Why did I always sound so lame?

The annoying bells grated the air. For the millionth time.

I glanced up to see an attractive guy walk in alone. I searched for something else to clean, not in the mood to deal with anybody, especially good-looking anybodys.

"Hey, Bryce." I motioned him over to the counter. "Help that guy when he's ready. I'm going to start closing up in the back so we can get out of here early."

He grinned. "I like the sound of that."

I scurried into the supply room, applauding myself for my quick thinking. Bryce had smiled. That meant I wasn't as intimidating as Mr. Owens suspected. Honestly, I didn't have an intimidating bone in my body. Only timid ones. But managers had to be assertive, so I pretended, in order to excel at my job. I must have overcompensated.

Bryce stuck his head around the door as I stacked bins in the freezer. "Meridee, that guy up front wants you."

"H-he wants a manager?" Dealing with angry patrons made me break into hives.

See, Mr. Owens, I wanted to scream, *I'm not intimidating. I'm intimidated.*

"No. He wanted me to find the cute girl who was just out there so he could talk to her." He winked. "I think you have an admirer."

"Oh, go away." I shooed him. "I'll be there in a second."

I shook my head when the door closed. Bryce liked to tease. I couldn't take anything he said seriously. I pulled my shoulders back and marched out to where the cute customer waited at the counter.

I swallowed to moisten my throat. "I'm the manager. Did you need to see me?"

He gave me a crooked smile. "Yeah. Hi. I'm Riley Kirkpatrick."

When he said nothing more, I squeezed my fingers. "Bryce said you needed me. What can I help you with?"

He shifted his weight to the other foot. "You don't know me." He winced. "Well, I guess you know my name now." He gave me another lopsided grin.

My smile was seconds away from cracking. I wished he'd spit it out and get to the point. Did he have a complaint or not?

"I came in here the other day and ordered ice cream." He wrinkled his nose. "Of course, I ordered ice cream, right? It's an ice cream shop." He chuckled, sounding nervous. "You probably don't remember." He raised his brows, as though he hoped I did.

I frowned, thinking he meant I didn't remember this was an ice cream shop, which was totally untrue. But then I realized he was asking if I remembered him. Duh.

My cheeks burned. Talking to cute guys made me super uncomfortable.

"Sorry. Lots of people come through here. Everyone blurs into each other after a while." Though it surprised me that I couldn't remember him. He had cuteness out the wazoo. "Was there anything wrong with it?" I asked. "Your ice cream?"

"Oh, no." He shook his head. "It was great. Delicious, actually. I've never been here before, but my buddy texted to meet him here. He left before I could—" He waved his hand. "Never mind that. My ice cream was amazing. The best ever."

My muscles relaxed. He hadn't come to complain and make my job difficult. "I'm glad you enjoyed it."

He scratched his throat as the bells rang. Glancing over his shoulder, he turned back to me and blurted, "What's your name?"

If he hadn't been so adorably nervous, I might have worried he was a stalker. He still might be.

But I gave him the answer he sought. "Meridee."

"Meridee," he repeated. "That's pretty."

"It's weird."

A family pushed in behind him. He motioned them forward. "Go ahead."

The kids squeezed up to the counter, mashing their faces against the glass. No wonder I always had to clean the thing.

The dad gestured to Riley. "Take your time, son. We'll be a while."

Riley's forehead scrunched as he pointed to the first bin. "I'll have a single of Cougar Tracks in a cup."

Grateful he'd made up his mind, I grabbed the scooper and went to work. When I met him at the cash register, words rushed out of his mouth.

"Would you like to go out with me Saturday night, Meridee?"

I touched my parched throat. "M-me?"

He nodded. "That's why I returned. I tried to have your coworker get you from the back last time, but he said you were busy."

I blinked. He'd come earlier? And he wanted to go out? What the hay? Things like this didn't happen to me, not since...

I shook my head. "I-I guess so."

Please let him not be a stalker.

He pushed a napkin across the counter. "Write your address and phone number. I'll call you with details." He seemed happy, giddy even.

I wrote down my info, wondering why he didn't enter my number into his phone like a normal person.

He stuffed the napkin into his wallet and grinned. "Thanks, Meridee. I'll see you Saturday."

"Okay." I rubbed my forehead as he turned to leave.

Who had stolen my invisibility cloak?

I wanted it back.

8

PARKER

THE OVERPOWERING SMELL of sweat, soap, and stinky cleats made me wince. I toweled off and retrieved my clothes from my locker. The offensive coach had made me put in extra time at the weights, after reviewing hours of reels in preparation for the upcoming game. I was hammered, but still had a long night ahead of me—reviewing for my upcoming physics test, finishing a paper for business writing, and meeting Lily and the guys.

I rubbed my throbbing head, wishing to skip out on that last part. Not because I didn't want to see Lily, but because I was dead on my feet. But I must keep my woman happy. She'd already given me grief for studying too much and ignoring her.

Dating a goddess had its drawbacks.

Riley approached as I pulled on a pair of sweats.

"Hey man," I said.

"Hey." He shuffled his feet. "Great job out there today. You were on fire."

"Thanks." I wanted to say, *You too*, but Riley had stunk it up on the field today. "What are you still doing here?" The other guys had left over an hour ago.

He twisted the strap on his duffel bag. "I wanted to see if..." He scratched his head.

"If what?"

He stared at his shoes. "If you might want to double with me next

Saturday? I asked this girl and..." He shifted his weight back and forth. "Thought maybe we could go miniature golfing and catch a movie."

That sounded lame after the rocking parties I'd attended lately. But as I watched him fidget, I knew I needed to accept. Riley was shy and awkward with the ladies. He needed a wingman. And I owed him for ditching him last week at Ferdinand's.

I pulled on a sweatshirt. Being accepted by the "in" crowd had boosted my confidence. Maybe I could lift Riley's. I stuffed my towel in my bag and zipped it. I had a feeling miniature golf was beneath Lily. And so was my friend. She didn't like Riley for some reason. But he needed me.

"Mini-golf sounds fun," I said.

"Will you bring Lily?" I could tell by how he asked that he hoped not. He didn't seem to care for my girl. Maybe he was jealous.

"Duh," I said, trying to make him laugh. "She's my girl. Who else would I take?"

Riley looked down. "Oh, okay." He made a face. "How are things going with her?"

"She's amazing. I swear she has a double-doctorate degree in kissing."

"Probably because she has so much practice," he grumbled.

Yep. He was jealous.

"Let me text Lil to make sure her schedule's open next Saturday." Lily's planner was usually filled weeks ahead.

I sent her a text. Hers came back a minute later.

I frowned. "Aw shucks. She's already busy. Guess I can't come."

Riley's shoulders slumped, making me feel as though I was abandoning him again.

"Maybe I could bring someone else. Not a date. Just a space-filler, so our numbers are even."

Riley looked up, hopeful. "You'd do that for me?"

Kind of had to now since I'd gotten his hopes up. "Of course."

"That would be awesome. Let's meet at Airway Hills at six. We'll pick a movie afterward."

"Sounds good," I lied.

After Riley left, I sank onto the bench and hit my head against the locker. What had I gotten myself into? Now, I had to round up a friendly, platonic space-filler before next Saturday...and I had to keep Lily from finding out about it.

I sighed. The things I did in the name of friendship.

41

9

MERIDEE

*L*EANING AGAINST THE counter, I stretched my calves as I filled the hot fudge container. The bells from hell jingled, making me glance up from my work. I tensed and ducked below the counter when Parker Harrington entered the shop.

One of my coworkers could take his order.

"There you are," he said a few seconds later.

I lifted my head to find him stretched over the counter watching me. How humiliating. I raised my rag to the stainless steel, wiping an imaginary trail of something sticky. His striking blue eyes twinkled as though he found something funny.

Probably me.

"Here I am." I stood and slid over to the ice cream display. "What flavors do you want today, Sticky Fingers? I know you don't mind eating expired tubs. Should I check the dumpster for your favorites?"

He threw me one of his Kryptonite smiles. "I'm not here for ice cream. I need to watch what I eat until the big game tomorrow night. Are you going?"

I twisted the rag between my fingers. "Football's not really my thing. If I want to watch boys hit each other, I'll go to the early childhood preschool on campus and observe through the windows for free."

His mouth fell open. "Have you watched *any* of my games?"

"No." I rubbed my neck. "You have your cheerleaders and the rest of the student body willing to watch and stroke your already inflated ego."

He chuckled. "You're missing out, Mare."

"Meridee," I corrected. "Only my friends call me Mare."

He reached out and grabbed my hand. "Meridee, I wondered if you'd be up for mini-golf and a movie next Saturday night. To make up for that mishap in the CUB."

I blinked but couldn't form words. In fanciful daydreams, I'd imagined him holding my hand, but never had I expected it to happen. Holy llama. Parker was an electrical socket, sending a steady stream of tingling energy pulsing through my connected hand.

And wait! Had he just asked me out?

I was still playing catch-up. Didn't he already have a girlfriend?

I whipped my hand away from him. "No, thanks." I rubbed the shiny counter to conceal a blush. For a moment, I'd thought he was serious. "You don't have to make up for anything. Let's forget that incident ever happened."

"Oh, come on. I'm in a bind and need a date, and you could use some fun in your life."

I scowled. What did he mean by that?

"I don't bite." He playfully chomped his teeth. "And I've stopped playing football in the CUB and tackling girls to the floor. You've had a reforming influence on me, Mare."

I narrowed my eyes. "It's Meridee."

"Come on. Say you'll go with me, Meridee. We'll have a blast."

I tucked my arms into my side. "I can't."

"Why not? Do you work?"

"No. I get off early that night."

"Then you *can* go." He leaned over the counter and waggled his brows.

No wonder he wasn't used to hearing no. When not tackling girls to the floor, he could be very persuasive.

I continued my needless scrubbing. "I already have a date."

"Cancel it. Surely he's not as great a catch as me."

"I can't cancel on my fiancé." I crossed my fingers, hoping that whopper might stay his pity.

"You're engaged?"

His disbelieving tone whacked my ego. I nodded.

"No way. I've been coming here forever and have never observed a guy anywhere near you. If you were *engaged*"—he made quote marks in the air—"I'd have noticed a guy hanging around."

"That's the thing," I said, wishing I'd kept my mouth shut. Every time I lied, I made things worse. "Your big head makes it impossible to see outside of you."

"Prove it."

"What? That you have a big head?"

He smirked. "Call your fiancé. Tell him there's this hot jock making moves on you." He flexed a bicep and made a sizzling noise between his teeth. "I'll wait here until you introduce him to me."

"Are you in junior high?"

He put his hand to his ear. "Call him."

The bells rang, bringing in a group of teenagers. One of the boys spotted Parker and yelled, "Whoa! You're Sticky Fingers."

Parker lifted a hand to acknowledge him but gave me a double eyebrow lift. "I'm waiting." When I glared, he leaned over to whisper. "Call your man, or I'll know you're lying and be by to pick you up Saturday night. Tara told me where you live." His blue eyes crinkled at the corners.

Tara had what?

I folded my arms. "Fine. I'll call him."

"I can't wait to meet your soul mate."

I stomped into the break room and sent Danny out to handle the teenage rush with Bryce.

Soul mate. What a moron.

I pulled out my phone and hit speed dial. On the third ring, my big brother answered.

"What's up, Mare?"

"Thanks for answering." I released the breath I'd been holding. "I need a huge favor."

"Name it, sis. You know I'm here for you."

I frowned at the pity in his voice. But pride had no place at the moment, not with Parker Harrington waiting in the shop. "There's this guy bothering me at work. Stalking me," I lied. If he suspected danger, Mark would rush right over. "Can you come over and pretend to be my fiancé so he'll leave?"

"Want me to just kick his trash?"

"No. This guy's way bigger than you. He'd stomp you into the ground. Please, Mark. I just need him to see that I'm already taken. Then he'll leave."

"You don't expect me to hold hands or kiss you, do you?"

"Don't be a dweeb. Just get over here and let me introduce you to him.

He doesn't believe I have a boyfriend."

"You don't."

I gnashed my teeth. "That's why I need your help."

"When are you going to date again, Mare?" Concern dripped from his voice. "Not all guys are jerks. It's been over three years."

I closed my eyes. "I actually do have a real date next Saturday and don't want this guy ruining it. So will you help or not?"

"Okay, fine," he moaned. "But remember, no PDA."

As if I'd want to kiss my brother. "You're a moron."

I hung up on his snorting laughter and returned to the counter. When Parker waved from across the room, I averted my head.

Mark couldn't get here fast enough.

Ten minutes later, my brother sauntered into the shop. I took off my apron and hung it on a peg.

"Hey, Bryce. I'm taking my break."

He waggled his brows and made a kissy face as he glanced over at Parker.

I scowled at the tease, before walking out to meet my brother. Mark stiffened when I hugged him.

"Try to act as though you like me," I whispered.

He wrinkled his nose and took my hand like it was bleeding. "So where's your stalker?"

I led him to Parker's table and lifted our clasped hands. "Uh, Parker?" I maintained eye contact to feign confidence. "This is Mark, my fiancé." Heat crawled up my neck and into my cheeks as I squeezed my brother's hand. "Mark, h-honey." I cleared my throat, feeling beyond awkward. "Parker here didn't believe that—"

"Hey," Mark dropped my hand and stepped closer, a huge grin on his face, "you're Harrington, the wide receiver on the team. Number sixteen, right?"

Parker nodded at my imbecile brother.

"You have a huge game tomorrow, man. Are you ready?"

Parker shrugged. "As ready as I'll ever be." He reached out to shake hands with my brother. "What's your last name, Mark?"

I shook my head at my brother. If Parker had asked Tara where I lived, maybe he'd squeezed other details out of her as well, like my surname of Mansford.

"Mans-uh-ly," Mark stammered, catching my head shake at the last moment.

"Mark Mans-uh-ly," Parker repeated with a goofy grin. "How long have you two been engaged?"

"Just barely," I said as Mark blurted, "About three months."

Oh, kill me now. Mark was the worst fiancé ever.

My brother snorted. "Go with Meridee's answer. I'm a guy and don't keep track of dates. Feels like forever though, snookums."

I resisted the urge to roll my eyes.

Parker's dimple appeared and his eyes got a mischievous glint. Did he suspect us?

"Where are your rings?"

Of course, he did.

This time, my brother let me answer.

I latched onto his arm. "Mark gave me his grandmother's ring, but it didn't fit. The jeweler's resizing it."

"Yeah." Mark shrugged, trying to get rid of my hand. "I didn't realize girls had different size fingers."

I pinched his hairy arm. "You're silly."

Parker stood, dwarfing my brother. "It's nice to meet you, Mark Mans-uh-ly." He stuttered the name as Mark had done and patted his shoulder. "You have a great gal here. Mare makes the best triple decker waffle cones ever, but I'm sure you already know that." He saluted me. "Later, future Mrs. Mans-uh-ly."

Parker turned to leave, and Mark released my hand as though it contained a biological weapon. "Good luck tomorrow, man. I'll be cheering for you."

Parker turned to study us.

I latched onto Mark's arm and rubbed it. When he stiffened, I wanted to jab him. Did he have to act quite so disgusted? It wasn't as though this was any easier for me. Rubbing his arm was like petting Chewbacca.

"With Meridee?" Parker asked.

Mark wrapped an arm around my shoulder and squeezed, making me wince. "Of course, with Meridee. We watch all your games, don't we, sweetie pie?" He punched his other hand in the air. "Win the day for Crimson and Gray. Best in the West. Go, Cougs!"

I stomped on my brother's toe but the damage was done.

Parker winked at me. "You two lovebirds have fun. Enjoy the *game*, Mare."

The infuriating man chuckled all the way out the door.

46

PARKER

SECOND THOUGHTS WALLOPED me as I pulled into the parking lot. I knew Riley wouldn't be happy to see Lily, but when that Meridee from the creamery had turned me down because of a bogus fiancé, I'd begged Lily to do me this favor to help Ry out.

"Mini-golf?" Lily huffed.

I had conveniently forgotten to tell her what we'd be doing. No way she would've agreed to come if she'd known.

A group of junior high teens crossed the parking lot, shoving and pushing each other like they'd just eaten a truckload of cotton candy.

"It was Riley's idea." I gave her my best sad puppy impression. "I promise to make this up to you, babe."

"You'd better." She scowled and began texting.

"Hey, it'll be fun because we're together."

She gave me a look that clearly said, *Are you kidding me?*

I knew this had been a bad idea.

"You owe me big time," she said as I helped her out of my truck.

What was new? I always owed her for something—spending too little time with her, planning lame dates, not being home when she came over, talking to other girls, though that hadn't been my fault. They'd stopped me to ask for my autograph. I hadn't flirted or anything. I really wished for my sweetie back, the girl who'd been so cuddly and accommodating a few weeks ago. But that girl had totally disappeared.

Inside the noisy venue, I spotted my friend by a drinking fountain. I paused midstride when I recognized the girl beside him. I blinked and looked again, but I wasn't seeing a mirage. Meridee from the ice cream shop really, truly stood there, holding Riley's hand. And she looked hot.

"Hey, Parker," Riley said. "This is my date, Meridee Mansford."

I held out a hand. "Nice to meet you, Meridee. Can I call you Mare?"

Spots of color dotted her cheeks as she glanced at everything but me. "No, you may not."

Her obvious discomfort made me smirk. "This is Lily Meyers." I wrapped my arm around her. "My girlfriend."

Lily leaned up to kiss my cheek. "You're so adorable."

Outside on the course, Riley took Mare's hand again. "I thought we'd play couples. Whoever loses buys ice cream."

Lily wrinkled her nose. "Whose lame idea was it to play mini-golf?"

Riley ducked his head and turned three shades of red.

"I think mini-golf's super fun." Meridee's smile erased the shame from my friend's face, and I loved her for sticking up for him.

Lily scoffed. "You would." She narrowed her eyes. "You work at that ice cream shop on campus, right?"

Now, poor Meridee turned bright red as she squirmed. "Yeah."

"I'm glad to see you're wearing foundation, although you need a different shade. That one doesn't match your skin tone at all. You have a line at your neck."

I cleared my throat, feeling way uncomfortable. "It's your turn, Lil." I shoved the putter into her hand. When she stepped up to the ball, I turned to Meridee. "Don't listen to her," I whispered. "I think you look great."

Meridee stepped to the other side of Riley.

He gave me a pointed look as he tipped his chin toward Lily. "I thought you said you weren't bringing her."

"Sorry. I couldn't find anyone else." He might cut me some slack if he knew I'd tried to bring his date.

When it was her turn, Meridee whacked the ball instead of tapping it, making me wonder if her comment in the beginning about loving mini-golf had been a stretch.

Lily laughed as Mare's ball sailed out of sight.

"Wow!" I teased, before Lil could say something mean. "What did that ball ever do to you?"

Meridee glared at me. So much for teasing. She seemed to hate me.

Lily's gaze flickered to Mare. "Where did you get that sweater? It's so retro." Retro had never sounded so demeaning.

Riley pushed between the two girls.

"It's cool," I said to Meridee, earning a nasty glare from Lil.

The game took for-freaking-ever. After Lily and I kicked Riley's and Meridee's trash, we drove to the Village Center Cinemas.

Lily pouted. "What's with your fixation with that ugly ice cream worker?"

My hands tightened on the wheel. "I'm not fixated on her. And she's not ugly."

"You think she's pretty?"

I rolled my eyes. "She doesn't compare to you, Lil." No girl did.

"You disagreed with everything I said. I was just trying to give her style tips, which she needs. I've never met anyone so dowdy."

I was surprised Lily even knew that word. "Your tips came off kind of hurtful."

"Why do you care? Do you wish you were with her, instead of me?"

I glanced over at her and snorted. "Don't be ridiculous."

She pouted. "I do you a favor and this is how you repay me, by ogling other girls and jumping down my throat for trying to be nice. I didn't want to go miniature golfing, you know? And a movie? Seriously! Have we reverted to junior high? We could've hung out with Jacob and the guys. Why did you agree to hang out with that loser?"

"He's not a loser. Riley's my friend."

She flipped her hair over her shoulder, and we drove the rest of the way in silence.

At the theater, I led her inside and settled myself between her and Meridee, not wanting to give Lil a chance to give Meridee anymore *beauty tips*. When the previews began, Lily excused herself to use the restroom. Probably to reapply makeup or text friends. She'd hardly put her phone down all night. I knew she was ticked, and I felt bad for roping her into this fiasco. I'd known she would hate everything about tonight, but I'd hoped that for me, she would make the best of it. Heavens knew I'd spent many nights with her friends dealing with the boredom the best I could.

Since Lil had ditched me, I nudged Mare. "Who was the chump the other night and how much did you pay him to act like your fiancé? I hope it wasn't much, because his acting sucked. Your's, too."

"Shush. I don't have to tell you anything."

I let my hand creep under the armrest above her knee. "Tell me or I'll make you jump and claw the ceiling."

I barely squeezed and her hand clenched mine. "Stop!" she hissed. "It was my brother, okay?"

I released her knee and threw more popcorn in my mouth. "I knew he couldn't be your boyfriend."

"You're so smart."

I palmed another handful of popcorn as Lily returned. She cuddled close and started nibbling my ear. Maybe she'd finally forgiven me. I closed my eyes to enjoy her ministrations.

When I opened them again, Riley was doing the age-old arm-stretch maneuver, yawning to get closer to his date. *Go, Ry!* I wanted to yell in support. Meridee had surprised me tonight with how well she'd cleaned up. She looked freaking amazing, not that I'd ogled her as Lily had accused earlier.

I gritted my teeth. For as beautiful as Lily was, she was surprisingly super insecure. I knew from a passing comment she'd made that her dad had abandoned her and her mom when she was younger. Maybe she still had issues from that.

I wrapped an arm around her, hoping to assure her I wasn't like her dad. I wasn't going to leave her, like her dad had done. And I wasn't a player, like Carsen...or her chump ex-fiancé. She had no reason to be jealous of other girls.

Halfway through the movie, Lily leaned closer. "Abbi's calling. I'll be back in a few."

I gaped at her as she scooted out of the row. Why couldn't she put her phone away and relax? Her phone seemed welded to her hand. Even when we were together, she couldn't stop taking selfies of us or carrying on text conversations. She never was truly present, I realized.

Ry took off to refill his Coke, leaving Mare and I alone. How could anyone leave mid-movie? I didn't get it.

I leaned over to whisper. "Will you let Riley-boy kiss you when he takes you home?"

"None of your business."

I knew it wasn't, but Riley probably wouldn't kiss her on his own. He was major awkward with the ladies. And Meridee seemed shy as well.

I nudged her. "I think you should give him a peck. He's a super good guy, but he's shy."

"Like you?"

I snickered. "Funny."

Lily returned but kept checking texts, oblivious to the movie. Or me.

I reached over with my free hand to squeeze Meridee's knee, making her yelp and jump halfway out of her seat. Popcorn spilled all over the floor.

I kept a straight face as Lily leaned forward to glare at her. "Quiet." Under her breath, she muttered, "Dork."

I winced. That had seriously backfired. Why was Lily in such a bad mood? I knew she hadn't liked mini-golf and didn't seem interested in the movie, but couldn't she be happy to be with me? I'd gone to several parties with her I wouldn't have chosen, but I'd had fun because we'd been together.

I lifted my Coke, but Meridee chose that moment to reap revenge. Her pointy elbow dug into my side, making soda spew from my mouth into the empty seat in front of me and Lily to the side.

Lily gasped and jumped to her feet. I don't know if it was a knee-jerk reaction, or if she was aiming, but her hand smacked my face as she lashed out with equally stinging words. "Idiot! Look what you've done."

She muttered swear words as she pushed down the aisle.

I don't know what came over me, but I bent over and shook with silent laughter. Never had I expected Meridee to return tit for tat. But boy howdy, did she know how to get even.

I leaned back in my seat and grinned. Lily would no doubt kill me for spitting soda all over her name-brand clothes, but right now, I didn't care. Meridee's jab had released the tension that'd knotted me up inside. I loved being treated so normal. Maybe if she kept dating Riley, we'd see more of each other.

And I'd get even.

"You'd better go check on your Barbie," Meridee said.

I snorted at her description of Lily. But she was right. I left the theater and found Lily fuming in the lobby.

"I will not have you flirting with that loser girl in front of me!"

I stared at her. "What are you talking about?"

"You don't think I know what's going on?" She raised her hand to slap me, but I caught her wrist and led her outside. One slap was enough for the night.

I opened the passenger side door for her.

"Where are you taking me now?" she said. "That cheesy ice cream shop you like?"

"I'm taking you home." I couldn't take anymore drama. Maybe it was her time of the month. I hoped her black mood could be blamed on something normal like that. Something we could laugh about in a few days.

"So you can come back here and hook up with that freckled bimbo?"

"Lil, Meridee is Riley's date. I'd never flirt with my best friend's girl. I'm not a player."

"You could've fooled me."

Maybe I was the one who'd been fooled. We'd only been a couple for a few weeks...and I was exhausted. Were all relationships this hard? I loved Lily. I did. But she messed with my equilibrium. One minute, she made me soar to the heavens as we kissed, the next I wanted to cringe because of something she said to someone. The next, she'd be flirting with another guy, making me jealous. And two minutes later, I'd feel on top of the world and forgive her everything.

Tonight had been a disaster. From the minute I'd picked her up, Lily had been annoyed, put out, irritated, and unapologetically disgusted by what I'd asked of her. I hadn't been able to do anything right, though I'd tried. She'd been downright rude to my friends. She'd snubbed me during the movie. And she'd accused me of being a cheater.

I wanted to shake her and tell her to grow up and be nice. But I swallowed hard and drove to her place in silence. Deep down, I didn't want to make things worse.

FRIEND ZONE

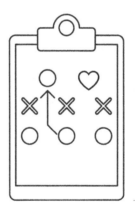

11

MERIDEE

*F*ERDINAND'S WAS HOPPING. One of the children in the family ordering licked his ice cream off his cone and onto the checkered floor. His high-pitched wail added to the chaos. This scene happened more than I liked. The mother picked up her sobbing child and grabbed napkins from a tin holder.

"Don't worry," I said. "I'll make him another and clean up the mess."

"Thank you." She gave me a frazzled smile.

"Bryce," I called, "bring a mop up front."

I scooped and smashed the ice cream tighter into the cone, before handing over the resurrected cookies and cream to the mother to give her red-eyed boy.

The annoying bells rang again, and Parker and Riley entered. I hid a smile as Riley waved. We'd gone out twice more since our double-date with Parker and his horrid Barbie. Riley was a nice guy. But we both had busy schedules, so he stopped by to say Hi on his way to or from practice if I was working. Parker tagged along. He was actually a nerdy goofball under that cool kid mask he wore. He made me laugh a lot, which made our time together way more comfortable than if Riley came alone.

I patted my face, hoping the foundation hid my freckles.

Parker raised a hand. "Hi ya, Meridee."

Customers turned to gawk. Why did he have to be so loud and single me out now that I dated his best friend?

"Hey." I finished making the rest of the family's orders. Out of the corner of my eye, I observed one of the older boys tug at his dad's shirt and point to Parker.

"Hey, kid." Parker knelt to be eye-level with him. "You like football?"

The boy stared up at him and nodded as though Parker was Captain America. Parker patted his head and started chatting about the dumb game he loved. When he produced two tickets from his pocket and waved them in front of his star-struck fan, the boy's eyes widened.

"I happen to have two tickets to next Friday's game. Any chance you and your dad want to go?"

The boy's head almost fell off his neck as he nodded.

I smiled. Parker was super sweet.

He patted the kid's moppy hair and handed him the coveted tickets.

"Thank you so much, Sticky Fingers," the father said.

I shook my head at the moronic nickname that didn't fit him at all.

"My pleasure. You guys have fun at the game."

Riley sauntered up to the counter, and my coworkers gave me knowing grins and backed away so I could take his order. I tuned out Parker's fan club and met Riley's gaze, feeling myself get warm all over. Two nights ago, at the end of our third date, he'd kissed me. Now, I didn't know how to act around him. Would he expect a kiss every time he saw me, even on breaks?

I clenched the counter.

"How's your day going, Meridee?"

"Good. What about yours?"

"Practice was rough. I need an ice cream to soothe my battered ego."

"That bad, huh?"

He shrugged. "Sometimes I wonder why I show up for practice. As third-string safety, I know I'll never play."

"That has to be tough." I shifted my weight, wondering what a third-string safety was. Maybe some sort of concussion rule that kept him on the bench? I wished he'd order and leave so I could breathe again. Cute boys stressed me out.

When my fingers started tingling, I relaxed my grip on the counter. "What can I get you?"

"What would you recommend?"

I wrinkled my nose. Why was conversing with guys so difficult? Shouldn't it be getting easier to talk with him, not harder? "I don't know. Everything tastes the same to me after working here so long."

"Get the huckleberry." Parker slapped his friend's back and waggled his brows. "Hey, Mare. Sexy hat."

"Shut up." I self-consciously adjusted the dumb hat Mr. Owens had insisted we start wearing to look more professional. Why couldn't he have picked regular caps, instead of these outdated paper things that resembled a sailboat?

Bryce and Susan snickered behind me.

I turned to scowl at them. "Why don't you two fill the topping bins?" Facing forward, I came nose to nose with Parker, who'd pushed Riley out of the way. "You're super cute when you're bossy."

I grabbed my scoop and turned my back to him to hide my flaming face and overwrought heart. "And you're super annoying." I took a deep breath and faced Riley. "Choose whatever you want. It's on me."

"Ah. You're sweet." He gave me one of his crooked half-smiles. "I guess I'll try the huckleberry ripple."

Parker leaned over again to steal the attention. "Make that two, except I want mint chip and chocolate peanut butter as well."

I pointed my scoop at him. "Yours isn't on the house, Mr. Greedy-Pants." My whole face heated again at how lame I sounded.

"Riley's paying for mine."

"What?" Riley turned to stare at him. "No, I'm not."

"Yes, you are." Parker grinned. "Remember our bet about whether Mare would come to the game after you kissed her? She didn't, so I won."

I propped a hand on my waist. "You made a bet about kissing me?"

Riley turned scarlet. "Sorry."

"What about you?" I glared at Parker.

He smirked. "I'm not sorry. I won an ice cream out of it." He tapped my clenched hand. "Make my scoops extra big, would ya? I worked up an appetite at practice."

I grabbed a sugar cone for Riley and made his treat as a group of coeds entered and surrounded Parker, squealing and throwing their self-respect at him like Hawaiian leis on a tourist. Gag. Yes, Parker was hot with his piercing blue eyes, dark hair, and Nordic godlike features. Throw in his muscular bod, and he became almost worthy of worship. But did they need to act so desperate?

I handed Riley his single scoop.

"Thanks, Meridee." He chewed his lip. "Sorry about the bet."

"It's fine. I was kidding." Kind of. But Riley took everything so seriously that I didn't want him to feel bad.

Parker extricated himself from his fan club to jog over and hold the door for two old ladies who were hobbling up the outside walkway. He winked at the grandmas as they thanked him profusely.

"No problem, ladies." He gave them his winning smile. "Have you been here before? If not, you're in for a treat." He walked them to the line and kept talking as if they were his own grandmothers. The two sweet ladies giggled at his attention, and my heart melted. I'd missed seeing this side of him since he'd started receiving so much attention from fans.

He returned to the front as I scooped huckleberry ice cream.

"Don't be stingy," he said. "You know I'm your best customer. What will Mr. Owens think if you send me away hungry because you skimped on my scoops?"

I snorted at his dumb alliteration, making the irritating Boy Scout grin.

"Say that ten times fast. Now put it in a cup and fill in around the edges."

"Think again, buster. I'm not one of your sweet old ladies you can charm."

He stuck his lips out in a pout. "But Riley's scoop is bigger than two of mine combined."

He was such a liar.

"Because she likes me better than you," Riley jabbed, making me blush.

The coeds giggled louder from their spot in line, attempting to regain Parker's attention.

I held out his waffle cone. "Better go attend to your fan club."

"Don't remind me." He made a face and turned to wow them.

Riley handed me a five. "When's your break?"

"Let me whittle down this line."

"We'll wait outside for you, kay."

I licked my lips. "Okay."

When I walked outside about ten minutes later, the eyelash-batting coeds surrounded Riley's and Parker's table. I considered doing an about-face, but Parker spotted me and shouted.

"Mare, I saved you a seat."

I cringed as the girls gave me dirty looks. Parker was such a loud-mouth. Why couldn't he ignore me?

"I'll catch a touchdown for you next week, okay?" he told the girls. "Nice meeting all ya'll." Parker motioned for me to join him and Riley.

I stuffed my hands in my pockets. Riley stood and pulled me into a hug, which with my hands bound, felt super awkward.

"Is that huckleberry ice cream on your shirt?" Parker teased as I ended the hug-fest.

A maroon stain on my left breast almost sent me into cardiac arrest when I looked down and noticed it. Crap-tabulous!

Parker's beautiful fan club snickered and pointed.

"You should come to our party tonight, Sticky Fingers," one of them suggested. She wore a low-cut blouse and the shortest shorts ever.

Riley scooted over to make room for me. "Poor guy."

I inwardly rolled my eyes. Yeah, poor guy who had women throwing themselves at him wherever he went. I'm sure Parker just hated that.

"I'll see what I can do. Ya'll take care," he drawled, before diving into his melting cone.

"I don't envy you, man," Riley muttered.

"Me either," Parker said.

As much as I shunned the attention he received, I admired his friendly nature. When the other jocks had come with Lily, they'd been abrupt and even rude to a few fans who had dared approach them. But Parker never lost his smile. He made everyone—even two sweet old ladies—feel important and valued. Sadly, that probably inspired hope in too many coeds, including myself.

Riley grabbed my hand, making my whole body tense up.

I turned to Parker. "How's your cone?" Derp. Could I not think of anything better to ask?

"Amazing, like always." He winked.

My traitorous stomach fluttered, so I faced Riley. "So, uh, practice was hard?"

"Yeah. Coach ran us for over two hours." He squeezed my fingers.

"You can blame all the gassers we had to do on Swift. That idiot didn't make grades again." Parker pulled his cone away from his face, leaving a trail of mint chocolate chip above his lips.

Yum. My mind started fantasizing, even as I told it to behave and stop looking at those lips.

"Dude," Riley said, "you have ice cream under your nose."

Parker stuck his tongue out to lick it off, sending my thoughts into the naughty zone. What was wrong with me today? He winked at me, and I laughed. I couldn't help it.

Riley chuckled, too, but let go of my hand to take hold of my knee under the table.

I flinched as his fingers inched upward.

Parker grinned at us from his side of the table. "Let's play more of the Get-to-know-Mare game."

I rolled my eyes. "It's Meridee."

"Oops, I mean the Get-to-know-Meridee game."

"Let's not and say we did."

He ignored me. "Your mom's maiden name is Lincoln, but you're not related to Abraham. Your cat's favorite treat is Cheetos, and his name is Henry the Eighth because of his philandering ways. Seeing Hobbiton in New Zealand ranks at the top of your bucket list. What else do you have for us today?"

It surprised me the small details he remembered from past conversations. "Uh, my favorite drink is cream soda." I hated talking about myself.

Riley's hand inched higher, closing in on my thigh. "I love cream soda, too."

I gave him a weak smile, but could hardly breathe. Did he think that liking cream soda meant we were soul mates? I couldn't figure him out. Or rather, I couldn't figure me out. I liked Riley, although I wished he'd hold my hand instead of my leg. He was kind of freaking me out right now. I knew he was a gentleman because he'd asked permission before kissing me. I appreciated that more than he'd ever know. But I still didn't feel comfortable with his touch. I didn't know if that was due to my hang-ups or if I just didn't like him romantically. Parker constantly hijacked my attention and still played a major role in my dreams. Shouldn't Riley take over that job if he was my boyfriend?

"Are you free tomorrow night?" Riley whispered as he rubbed my thigh.

I shook my head. "I-I close. Then I need to study for anatomy." I inched over on the bench, putting distance between us. I'd rather not go out with him twice in one week. He might start having expectations, and I wasn't ready for intimacy. I wondered if I ever would be.

He leaned closer. "I guess I'll have to come by and see you on your break again."

"Sure, uh, that'd be nice." My smile felt like it might crack right off my face.

Riley could be defined by that word. Nice. He was a super good guy, like my brother. I had nothing against him. I even enjoyed his affection in private, although he'd never put a possessive hand on my thigh before today. I didn't like that. But the idea of kissing him in front of Parker made my stomach churn like a turbine engine.

"Hello?" Parker waved his hand in front of us. "Stop whispering sweet nothings to your lady, Ry. It's rude in company."

Riley moved his hand back to his lap. Thank you, Parker, for distracting him from my leg.

"Uninvited company doesn't count," Riley said.

Parker clutched his heart. "Uninvited? How can you say that, man? You practically begged me to come because you were scared Meridee might attack you."

I snickered into my hand. Like that would ever happen. Parker always said the craziest things.

Riley wrapped an arm around my shoulders. "I'd never be afraid of that," he whispered, making me blush again.

"Dude, you're doing it again." Parker tossed his napkin at us. "Hey, Mare."

"It's Meridee," I said automatically. My name had become somewhat of a joke between us.

"Meridee." Parker's eyes sparkled. "You work part-time at the hospital, don't you?"

"Yeah. I work an eight- or twelve-hour shift each week, depending on my schedule."

"Coach wants us to do community service. I wondered if you knew anyone there who could use some cheering up. I used to volunteer at a hospital in El Paso where my nephew stayed a few times, and I had fun reading stories and playing games with the kids."

I grinned so hard my cheeks hurt. If I hadn't thought he was perfect before, that comment won over my heart completely. Not that he'd ever know.

"There's a whole floor of kids who'd be ecstatic to have you visit. I work in the pediatric unit."

"Think you can set up a time for me and whoever else I can round up to drop by so you can put us to work?"

"I'm in." Riley reached for my hand under the table.

"I'll talk to my supervisor and let you know." I stood, still grinning. "Thank you. I better get back to work."

Riley stood to hug me. I grimaced as he gave me a chaste peck. "I'll call you after work."

I focused on the cement. "Okay."

"Don't eat too much ice cream on the sly," Parker teased. "Or cream soda. Riley doesn't want no five-hundred-pound girlfriend."

I laughed. Parker had made my day. Actually, he'd made my whole month. After working at the hospital for the past six months, I knew the value of volunteers. Especially famous ones who'd make certain kids' eyes shine again. I couldn't wait to broach his idea with Miriam tomorrow. She'd be thrilled.

Back in my spot behind the counter, I adjusted my derpy hat. If only Parker wasn't whooped by his brainless Barbie, he'd be absolutely perfect.

12

PARKER

*D*OWNING TWO MORE Tylenol, I grimaced. My right knee and shoulder still ached from the fall I'd taken in practice. I stretched my legs under the table and reached down to massage my kneecaps. It showed the sad state of my life that I sought refuge on the fifth floor of the library in a reserved group study room so no fans could find me...and a certain girlfriend.

Three weeks had passed since that disaster date with Riley and Meridee. Maybe Lily had been PMS-ing, because she'd been in a much better mood since. But my girl was high-maintenance, no doubt about it. Not that I was complaining. Well, maybe a little. At this point in my life—with football and senior level classes to ace—I didn't have lots of spare time to devote to her. And that caused major tension in our relationship. She wasn't nasty about it or anything, but I could just sense her dissatisfaction.

I rubbed my aching head. Maybe time would fix us. We were still in the get-to-know-each-other phase. I just needed to be more patient with her mood swings and figure out a way to carve more time out for her.

But not tonight.

Another text came in from Lily. The sixth. I swore under my breath, my vows to do better dissipating in frustration. Didn't she have her own classes to study for?

I took a moment to roll my stiff shoulder before calling her.

"Hey, Parkie." She answered on the third ring.

I hated her newest nickname. "What did you need, Lil?"

"I wondered where my sticky gummi bear had gone when I showed up at your place and you weren't there. Want to come home and hibernate together?" She started panting.

"Uh." I scratched my neck. Lily was a big tease. "I can't tonight. I have a huge physics test in the morning and another paper due in English."

She huffed. "You always have physics and English homework. If I didn't know better, I'd think you were cheating on me."

I closed my eyes to keep from screaming. We'd already talked about this. "Ah, Lil. You know you're the only woman for me. But I really have to do well on this test."

When she didn't respond, I pictured her sulking.

"After practice tomorrow, I'll take you to dinner. Anywhere you want. Afterward, we'll grab drinks at the Coug."

"How about John's Alley Tavern in Moscow?"

I winced. She always picked the clubs with the highest cover charges. "Fine." I guess I owed her since I couldn't hang out tonight. "I gotta go. See you tomorrow."

"Whatever. Go wrap yourself up in your homework. You never neglect it like you do me."

I ended the call and shook my head. Too bad Lil didn't share Meridee's work ethic. I'd never met anyone who worked and studied as hard as that girl did. I rubbed my hands together as I thought of helping out at the hospital tomorrow. Mare had set it up for Riley and me to come into the pediatric ward after lunch to play with the kids. I couldn't wait.

I opened my physics book and kept comparing both girls. Lil and Mare were night and day. Lily was the dazzling sun, so stunning and bright that everyone yearned to bask in her light. Her glowing confidence and stunning body had drawn me in like a moth to a flame. Meridee, in comparison, was the moon—beautiful in her own right, but in an understated way that could easily be overlooked. When Lily graced a room, Mare became invisible. But Lily could burn or scorch, whereas Mare had a soothing, calming effect. Like the tide, Mare was reliable and steady. Easy to be around. She didn't play games. Her every action made others feel good, like how she made my cones bigger and always gave me a cup for water without me asking, and how she complemented Riley and thanked him for opening doors or pulling chairs out for her.

I turned the page, trying to recall if Lily had ever thanked me for anything. She called me cutsie nicknames—Parkie, Gummi Bear, and a couple X-rated names that always made me blush. She gave kick-butt back rubs, but those usually led to me having to pick up and leave so I wouldn't cross a line she very much wanted me to cross. I couldn't recall her ever thanking me though for opening a door, taking her to dinner, or giving her flowers. She seemed to expect my devotion and gifts as her right.

My phone vibrated with another call, making me growl. Why couldn't she leave me alone for a few freaking hours?

I relaxed when I saw Mom's face on the screen, instead of Lily's glamour shot.

"Hey, Mom. What's up?" I leaned my chair back on two legs.

"How's my favorite boy?"

"Great. How about you? School treating you all right?"

"About normal. My class is full of a bunch of hooligans, but I'll tame them."

If she considered them hooligans, that meant half of them were in trouble with the law and on probation, and the other half hadn't been caught yet. Mom taught seventh grade English in an inner city, at-risk school in El Paso.

"I'm sure you will."

"That was a great catch in the third quarter. I couldn't be prouder."

I appreciated how she always watched my games and called or texted to rehash her favorite plays. "Ah, Mom, don't you know pride's a sin?"

"Yeah, so's false humility. Admit it. That was a good one. I don't know how you caught the ball with those two beasts on your back. When the ref pushed them off and you held up the ball, I thought the stadium might come unglued. How did it sound in person?"

"Loud."

She chuckled. "You're amazing, son. Your dad would be proud."

I scowled. "Next week's game against BSU will be a tough one. They've had a good season."

"Parker, your dad was a good man." She always knew when I was dodging unwanted conversations, dang it.

"I don't want to talk about him."

"Fine." She sighed. "What I called to tell you is I'm coming to your next game."

"What? You're coming to the BSU game? In person?"

She assured me she was, and I jumped up and down like a schoolboy pumped up for Christmas break.

"But how? Where did you get money for a flight?"

"I've been putting a few dollars aside for a couple years. Do you mind if I crash on your couch so I don't have to pay for a hotel?"

"You can crash anywhere. I'm so stoked." I wrote down her flight number and made arrangements to pick her up the following week.

Long after the call ended, I reflected on her news. We didn't see each other often enough. Mom used her meager school-teacher salary to support my two older sisters and their three kids. The oldest, my eight-year-old nephew Cody, had been born with a congenital heart defect and was in and out of the hospital. That's why I wanted to volunteer in the hospital here. It'd been way too long since I'd done something fulfilling. But with Cody's medical expenses and other life hiccups, there wasn't extra cash lying around for frivolous trips to football games, which made Mom's news epic.

Thinking of all she'd sacrificed over the years to keep our family together made me want to kick something. I hated Dad for leaving us like he had. Selfish bastard!

The clock on the wall showed that the library would soon close. Desperate for fresh air, I marched outside and headed to the parking lot.

I drove to Riley's apartment and let myself in. "Anyone here?" I called.

Riley stuck his head out from the back bedroom. "Yeah."

"Mind if I crash here for the night?" We could drive over to the hospital together in the morning that way.

He started coughing. "Make yourself at home. There's leftover chicken soup on the stove from Meridee and also homemade rolls."

"You sound awful."

He grunted and sank into a chair across from me. "Is Lily still hounding you?"

I blew on my soup. "You have no idea, man."

"Break up with her, dude. You don't need her drama."

"Nah, man. It's not like that. I just need some space tonight." She was my dream girl, but like a magnificent, wild stallion, she needed to be tamed.

Mare's soup slid down my throat, making me moan. "This is divine." I took another bite. "You know your girl is perfect, don't you?" She really was.

"She is." Another coughing fit bent him over. "I'm afraid I'll have to bail tomorrow. Meridee said she doesn't want me anywhere near her kids until I feel better." He coughed again.

"Probably a good call."

I devoured four of Mare's rolls and another helping of heavenly soup as I wondered what to do with Mom. If she stayed at my place, she might run into Lily. Heaven forbid. I doubted Mom's conservative nature was up for that. I'd have to gradually introduce the idea of Lily to her. But Riley's apartment would be too squished.

I tapped my spoon against my bowl. "My mom's flying out here for the BSU game."

"Cool."

"It's beyond cool. She hasn't attended a single college game of mine because of the distance. I'm stoked."

"That's great, man."

"But I need a place for her to crash, and someone to take her to the game so she won't have to sit alone." I chewed the inside of my cheek. "Think Mare could help me out?" When Ry frowned, my gut clenched. "She's just so chill. I know she'd get along great with my mom."

Riley tapped his fingers together. "Why not Lily?"

I squeezed my forehead, making him snort.

"Kidding. I'm sure Meridee would be fine with your mom crashing at her place. But I doubt she'd go to the game. You know how she hates football."

"That's the beauty of this. If I spin it right, how could she say no?"

He started coughing again. "Go for it. Who knows?" He shrugged. "Maybe you'll succeed where I failed and get her to a game."

"You don't mind if I steal her from you for a weekend?" No way would I ask Mare if Ry wasn't okay with it.

He headed to the sink to fill a mug with water. "Not at all. In fact, if you get Meridee to a game, I'll buy you dinner."

I pumped my fist in the air. "Now you're talking. Thanks, man."

He set his gray and black Raiders mug on the table and leaned over to cough into his shoulder. "Don't thank me yet. You still need to convince her to go. That'll be nigh impossible."

I rubbed my chin. Nothing was impossible.

13

MERIDEE

$\mathcal{W}$HERE WAS HE? I glanced at the clock and tried to ignore my queasy stomach. I'd fluffed pillows, locked wheelchairs in place, and joked around with some of the younger children for the last ten minutes as I waited for Parker to arrive.

He had to show. The kids were counting on him. So was I.

I knelt on the carpet to check on Paul. "Need anything, Pauly-popper?"

"How about a kiss, MD." The thirteen-year-old tease puckered his lips.

I patted his head. "Keep those lips to yourself, Pollywog."

Paul had been here for a few weeks as specialists kept testing, probing, and prodding him like a test subject to figure out what was going on with his body. He'd lost twenty-two pounds over the last two months and was rail thin, but he had the biggest heart of anyone I knew. Though his life sucked at the moment, he held fast to his silly sense of humor. In my limited experience, that'd do him more good than any medicine.

"Are you calling me a frog?" He waggled his brows. "Because they say you have to kiss a bunch of frogs before you find your prince. I'm more than willing to help you, Merrily on Your Way."

I rolled my eyes. Paul lived to think up new names for me. I tried my best to reciprocate. "I've given up on handsome princes, Paulyanna."

He huffed. "Don't you mean A-Paul-O 13?"

I laughed. "You're in for a treat today, space-boy." I fluffed his pillows. His ribs had started to ache over the last few days. I didn't want today's outing to set him back.

"Who's coming, Chickadee?" He winked.

I shook my head. "One clue, Pauly-pop. He's one of your favorite heroes." I glanced at the clock and prayed Parker would materialize. I'd told Riley to stay home because of his cold, but surely Parker would still come. I had nine anxious children waiting for something amazing to happen in their lives.

"Krusty the Clown?"

"You wish."

More minutes passed. My smile became stiff. If Parker didn't show, I'd wring his neck.

The door opened, and Parker entered in full football gear, carrying a helmet and ball. He glanced around the room. When he spotted me, he marched over to where I knelt beside Paul.

"Sorry I'm late." He panted. "My truck wouldn't start, so I had to run here since Riley had already left to go take a test and wasn't answering his phone."

I stared at him. "You ran all the way here?"

He took a deep breath. "Yeah, and obviously I'm not in as great shape as I thought because I'm beat."

I laughed. "And sweaty."

"Sorry."

"Don't be. I love you for still coming." I blushed and turned my back to him. Had I just said that out loud? "The kids have been getting anxious for their surprise."

"Sticky Fingers?" Paul said in an awe-filled voice.

"Yep." I patted Parker's padded shoulder. "Your hero has arrived." I turned to Parker. "This is Paul, your biggest fan."

Paul's cheesy grin validated my words.

Parker rubbed the boy's buzzed head. "Dude, nice to meet ya. What are you in for, and how much time have you served?"

I clapped my hands to introduce him to the rest of the kids. "Hey everyone, our special guest has arrived. This is Parker Harrington. He plays football for WSU. I've heard he's a pretty big deal."

"He's THE deal!" Paul corrected me. "He's Sticky Fingers."

"Yes, he is." I decided to tease him about the stupid name. "Be careful when you touch his hands so you don't get messy marshmallow or sticky syrup on you."

Parker pantomimed licking his hands and making them stick together like he couldn't pull them apart. He soon had all nine children in stitches—

the good kind that came from laughter. The kind that put life back into depressed hearts and disappointed souls. The kind that made my sick charges seem like normal kids for a moment. Parker seemed to be in his element as he joked and threw the ball back and forth with them. He let the kids take turns wearing his helmet, and even let Paul punch him a few times to prove his pads worked. My skinny charge was in heaven, especially when Parker had me take a picture of them together.

My supervisor stepped inside to check on us. Parker was on all fours, letting the children who weren't wheelchair-bound take turns tackling him.

"He's amazing," Miriam said.

"Yeah."

"Do you think you can get him to come back? The kids love him."

I loved him. "I hope so."

When it was time to get my charges back to their rooms, Parker winked at me. "When do you get off?"

"Actually, I'm off now. Want a ride home?"

"Please. I wasn't looking forward to the jog back uphill."

"Sorry about your truck, but thanks for still coming. You made their day."

He grinned. "They're pretty awesome." He glanced over at me. "So are you."

"Yeah, yeah." I downplayed his compliment, though I tingled from his words.

"You are. That Paul-kid is ready to marry you."

I laughed. Paul was ready to marry any girl that smiled at him. We reached my car and Parker hopped in the passenger side. I took a deep breath before getting in beside him. Never had I been alone with him. My heart beat double-time.

Parker started talking as we pulled out of the hospital parking garage. "My mom's flying up here next week for my game."

"That's nice."

"I haven't seen her since last Christmas."

Wow. He saw his family even less than I did.

"She's never been able to make it to one of my college games before."

"How long have you been on the team?" I'd pegged him for a junior or senior, but he must be younger if his mom had never watched him play yet.

"This is my fifth year. I red-shirted as a freshman." His brow furrowed. "She never missed a single high school game, even when she had to drive fifty miles to the next town to watch me. She's watched all of my broadcasted games but has never been able to attend in person." He cracked a few knuckles. "Anyway, I'm excited."

I stopped at a red light. "That's awesome."

"Yeah. So I have a favor to ask."

"Ask away." I felt surprisingly comfortable with him, which was odd. Even with Riley, I still tensed up and didn't know what to say when we were alone. But Parker and I were only friends. Riley wanted to be more. Maybe that made the difference.

He cracked more knuckles, making me cringe.

"The favor's not for me. It's for Mom. And Riley's okay with it." He pointed left. "Take me to Riley's. My stuff's there."

I knew where Riley lived since I'd taken dinner over to him last night. Parker grew quiet as I pulled into the complex.

"Would you mind waiting while I go change out of my gear? I'll buy you lunch."

"You don't have to do that." If anyone should be buying lunch, I should be buying his.

"I want to."

"Okay. Suit yourself."

He hopped out and jogged up the stairs. I destroyed my lips as I waited. What was I doing? I should've dropped him off and left, not wait so he could take me to lunch. That sounded like what a boyfriend would do.

Parker returned in cargo shorts and a red WSU shirt. Way too sexy.

I started breathing hard. We couldn't have lunch together. What if Riley found out? I was new to this whole dating thing, but surely going to lunch with his best friend wasn't kosher.

Parker climbed inside, making me frown. "Maybe lunch isn't the best idea. I should probably go up and see how Riley's doing." That's what a good girlfriend would do.

Parker shook his head. "Ry said to tell you hi. He was heading to his room to take a nap. I guess getting out to take that test took a toll on him."

My brow furrowed. "He knows we're going to lunch?"

He nodded. "Yeah. I told you he's okay with this. If he wasn't a walking germ bomb, I would've invited him along. No kissing Riley boy for a while."

"I didn't know that's something you did." My cheeks burned as I drove away.

Parker smacked my leg. "You know what I'm talking about, girl. No heavy make-out sessions until your boyfriend kicks this bug."

70

We stopped at a Subway, and he led me inside. Parker bought sandwiches and we walked outside to a table.

He reached across the space for my hand. "I have two tickets for next week's game, but since I'm playing, I obviously can't sit with my mom."

I gulped. The slight pressure of his fingers against my skin made my heart pound.

"I need someone to sit with her at the game. Also a place she can crash at for two nights. Preferably a girl's place." He raised both brows. "Can you help me, Mare?"

"It's Meridee."

"You said your friends called you Mare. And we're friends, right?" His fingers caressed my hand.

"I-I guess." The stroke of his thumb made me quiver like the strings of a violin under a master. Riley had never created such delicious harmony inside me.

He clutched his heart. "You guess? That hurts."

I shook my head at the tease. "Fine. You can call me Mare. You do anyway."

His winning smile appeared, melting my heart. "So, will you help me out, friend? Go to the game with my mom and let her stay with you?"

"Why me?"

He gave my hand a squeeze. "Because I think the two of you will get along."

"B-but she doesn't know me. You hardly know me. If you did, you'd know I'm socially inept." A dweeb. "Surely you can find someone not so awkward."

Parker ran his thumb across my knuckles, igniting a symphony. "You're adorable when you're flustered."

"I'm not flustered." Dang him and his blush-inducing powers. I pulled my hand away to silence the music. He might be a virtuoso, but he held the wrong violin.

His grin turned mischievous.

"Stop looking at me like that." I'd been doing so much better. Feeling more confident. Now, he'd shattered all my progress with a simple handhold and dumb question. When his lips twitched, I huffed. "I'm serious. I can't even carry on a conversation with my own mother. How do you expect me to talk to yours?"

His grin widened.

I pouted. "There are hundreds of gorgeous, confident girls dying to do you a favor. Ask one of them. Or your girlfriend."

He grabbed my hand again. "That's the thing, Mare. I don't want anyone else. You're down-to-earth and not fake like most girls. Mom will love you. She won't be able to help it."

I tugged my hand free and folded my arms. "But I hate football."

He laughed. "I know. Riley said he'd buy me dinner if I could get you to come. So please give a hungry guy a break and say yes."

I shook my head. Leave it to Parker to make a bet out of this.

He pushed his chair out and knelt in front of me. "Please, Mare. For my mom?"

Patrons at other tables craned their necks to watch us.

"Get up," I said. "Everyone probably thinks you're proposing."

He glanced around at the onlookers and wrapped his arms around my knees. "Please, oh, please, Meridee."

"Stop making a scene." I wobbled as I tried to step out of his grip.

He buried his head in my legs. "Say yes, Mare, or I'll die."

I smacked his head. Our audience had doubled, due to his theatrics. "Fine. Yes," I hissed. "Now let go."

Parker released me and jumped to his feet. Facing our not-so-subtle observers, he announced, "Today Meridee Mansford has agreed to"—he paused to draw out the suspense—"attend the game against BSU next week."

The crowd cheered. I tried to duck behind him, but he wrapped an arm around my shoulder and locked me in place.

"She's a junior and has never experienced a football game yet. Can you believe that?"

Several people gasped. Others chuckled. I wished for that missing invisibility cloak.

"Next week, I promise, on behalf of the team, that we will beat the Broncos, because not only will my mom be there"—he grinned as the crowd cheered again—"but Meridee as well. She's on her way to becoming my number one fan." He bowed.

I wrapped up my sandwich and marched to the car. "Do you want a ride home, or are you staying to do Act Two?"

He jogged over to join me but didn't say much on the drive back to Riley's. When I pulled up to the curb, he turned to me.

"Sorry. I didn't mean to embarrass you back there. You'll still take care of my mom though, right?"

I rolled my eyes. "Yes. I'll go to your stupid game, but don't be surprised if I bore her to death."

He grabbed my hand. As his thumb brushed across my knuckles again, my inner bowstrings hummed with a moving melody under the master's touch. I closed my eyes.

He had a girlfriend.

I had a boyfriend.

This soul-stirring music he created wasn't right. It was banned. Censored. Wrong.

"And will you also help me show her around that weekend?"

I blew out a breath, realizing the evocative music fell on deaf ears. He gazed at me with expectation, not yearning. I was making more out of this than he meant. Parker probably wasn't even aware that he still rubbed my hand.

"Greedy, aren't you?"

His dimple formed. "Maybe."

"Fine." He was my friend. I'd just keep my hands out of reach.

"Thanks, Mare."

I tugged against him, but he didn't release me. In fact, he brought his other hand to my cheek. I froze as the music crescendoed into an intense arrangement that left me weak and trembling.

"I miss your freckles." And *Bam!* whatever spell he'd put me under shattered as the music came to a screeching halt.

I ripped my arm away and scowled.

"Whoa!" He held up both hands. "What was that look for? I honestly think your freckles are cute. It's that concealer crap or whatever you call it that isn't attractive."

My jaw clenched. "I happen to be wearing that concealer crap you find so unappealing."

"Exactly. And you never did before Lily opened her big mouth. I'm just letting you know I liked you *au naturel.* Your freckles are cute."

"Cute is for puppies and girls in pigtails. It's not a compliment to a grown woman."

His Adam's apple bobbed. "But I like cute. Besides, you're not that grown. What are you? Maybe 5'2" tops?"

I narrowed my eyes. "I'm 5'3", thank you very much."

He chuckled. "Really, Mare. I didn't mean to offend." He cracked his knuckles.

I smacked his hands apart. "Stop doing that. Maybe we shouldn't be friends."

73

"What? I'm trying to make things right since Lily made everything wrong." When his face puckered like he'd swallowed a lemon, I raised one brow.

"Trouble in paradise?"

"If you call being smothered trouble, then yeah. I can't go anywhere without her latching onto me like a leech."

"Most guys wouldn't complain. She's very pretty."

"She's freaking gorgeous."

A surge of dissonant notes rushed through me. I forced a smile so he wouldn't sense my inner discord. "I'm sure you're the envy of every guy."

"I guess."

"You don't sound thrilled."

He took a deep breath and released it, making it difficult not to stare. His shirt clung to his chest, emphasizing muscles and giving my eyes a royal feast.

"Things have been tense between us. I want to fix our relationship but whenever I try, Lily distracts me."

"I don't even want to know what that means."

He squeezed his eyes shut. "It's just...oh, never mind." He tapped my nose. "I like your freckles. They're adorable. I won't take that back, even if it makes you huffy."

I huffed, making him snicker.

"And we are friends," he said firmly, but his eyes softened with a look that paused the dissonant inner music with a dramatic rest note.

I couldn't look away. I was powerless to move. My piano teacher growing up had taught me the power of silence in music, but never had I experienced the magic Mrs. Bauer swore a rest note contained until I gazed into Parker's deep blue eyes and glimpsed eternity.

"All joking aside, don't change because of what Lily said. She doesn't deserve your allegiance."

The rest note shattered. "I haven't given it to her." How dare he insinuate I cared what his bratty arm candy thought.

"Haven't you?" He brushed his hands across his nose and cheeks, referring to my irritating freckles.

I crossed my arms. "You're a sucky friend."

He laughed. "Don't schedule yourself to work next weekend."

I stuck my tongue out.

"You're the best, Mare." He pinched my chin, a sure sign that the music I'd heard had been only in my head.

14

PARKER

RAFFIC ON US-195 North moved fairly fast, but I couldn't say the same about conversation between Mare and me. I almost turned on the radio to banish the awkward silence, but that'd be the coward's route. I clenched the steering wheel, struggling to think of another question. Mom had flown into the Spokane International Airport instead of Pullman to save three hundred bucks. That meant instead of a fifteen-minute drive to pick her up, I had an hour and a half to kill in the truck with Meridee, since she'd agreed to make the trip with me.

"I still don't understand why you needed me to come with you," she said, not sounding happy.

"Company." I tilted my head to wink at her. "It's boring driving alone."

"You could've brought your girlfriend."

"Lily had some big cheer thingy tonight. Besides, this way you can meet my mom, instead of me just dropping her off like a total stranger at your apartment."

I pulled into the passing lane, noticing how stiff she sat, almost hugging the passenger door. From the moment I'd picked her up, Mare had been on edge. No matter how many jokes I'd cracked or funny stories I'd told, I hadn't succeeded in pulling a true smile from her. Was that because of the freckle comment last time? Maybe she hadn't appreciated my insight, but at least she'd listened. Her freckles weren't covered up today.

"How are things between you and Riley?"

She pushed a strand of hair behind her ear as her knee bounced. "We haven't dated that long."

They'd dated just a few weeks shorter than Lily and I. "Long enough for my friend to be smitten." I didn't blame him. Beneath Mare's serious exterior hid an amazing, kind, adorable girl who cooked, worked hard, cracked jokes, took care of people, and pulled off the whole girl-next-door sex appeal without even trying.

"He is not." She focused out the window.

"Is too." I changed lanes to pass a semi-truck. "Ry can't stop talking about you. Says you're a great kisser." I glanced over to gauge her reaction. Riley had never said a word about that, but I wanted to see what she'd say.

She blushed bright red. "We haven't kissed like that. We're taking things slow."

"Why? If you both feel the zing, get on the swing."

She snorted.

"I'm not joking. He really is crazy for you." Maybe he hadn't made it clear to her.

"Riley's sweet."

I winced. "You know guys hate being called sweet, right?"

"Like I hate being called cute?"

"*Touché*. But really, how do you feel about him?"

Her knee bobbed faster. "I don't know. It's been a while since I dated, so we're still in the awkward stage, which is probably my fault."

I'd observed how tense she became whenever Riley put a move on her. She laughed, joked, and smiled non-stop when the three of us bantered together, but the moment Riley wrapped an arm around her or made a flirty comment, she'd stammer, her smiles would become strained, and she'd appear ready to bolt.

"How long since you dated?"

She made a face. "A while."

I scratched my head, wondering how a girl like her hadn't been asked out every weekend. Meridee had cuteness out the wazoo. Guys appreciated that almost more than hot and steamy. I didn't care what she said about cute. Women like Lily intimidated and exhausted us. Of course, Mare did kind of hang back and act aloof, and nothing intimidated guys more than a girl who gave off chilly vibes.

"What about you?" she said. "How long have you dated Barbie?"

My lips twitched. "Lil and I have been together almost six weeks. But I've been in love with her for years."

Meridee fidgeted. "At the risk of sounding petty, I think you could do better. That girl's totally playing you."

I squeezed the steering wheel.

"When you brought her into Ferdinand's, I saw her hook up and kiss that other guy—the one who left you with the bill—while you ordered."

My jaw clenched. So Lily *had* messed around with Carsen after we'd gotten together. I tried to play it off like it didn't matter. To admit otherwise would paint me the fool.

"We weren't officially together then."

Meridee's knee kept beat to a silent punk rock song. "She's not very nice."

"She's actually very sweet. She didn't mean to hurt your feelings when she pointed out your freckles that one day. She considered it constructive criticism—which by the way, I don't agree with her. I'm glad you didn't cover them up tonight."

She blushed and fidgeted more.

"Tell me about your family." It was way past time to stop talking about my girlfriend. "I know you have a brother who must adore you, because he posed as your lame fiancé."

"Don't remind me."

I chuckled. "Tell me about him."

Her nervous knee bouncing ceased. "Well, his name actually is Mark. That part was true. He's in his last year of med school and waiting to find out where he'll do his residency."

"No kidding. He's a doctor?" I shook my head. "I'd never have guessed."

She finally smiled. "Mark's brilliant, but he dresses like a slob when not in scrubs. He's also an idiot about football. I'm afraid he kind of bro-crushed on you and couldn't give his fiancée adequate attention that day you met him."

I laughed.

She hugged her body. "He wasn't thrilled to play my boyfriend. My family isn't demonstrative—at all. Acting lovey-dovey almost killed him."

I snorted. "I should've asked you guys to kiss."

She batted my arm.

"Tell me about the rest of your family." That seemed a non-awkward topic. She seemed in a better mood, at least.

"My dad's an anesthesiologist. Mom's a CPA."

"Wow. Your family's successful."

She shrugged. "What about you? I know your mom's a schoolteacher. What about your dad?"

And *slam!* Conversation stalled again.

My knuckles turned white on the steering wheel. Mare was usually easy to talk to, but tonight we kept striking out. "He's dead."

"I'm so sorry," she whispered.

My lips pressed together. "Don't be. It happened long ago. I'm over it."

15

MERIDEE

*P*ARKER CUT OFF a blue Prius and screeched to a stop. I clutched the door handle, wishing I hadn't agreed to come. The long drive to Spokane had been beyond uncomfortable. We hadn't been able to keep a conversation going, like we usually could. I was disappointed that Parker couldn't see his girlfriend through clear lenses. He was totally blinded by her beautiful face.

Even when I'd revealed her two-timing ways, he'd brushed it off as unimportant. And now, I had a ninety-minute drive home to endure, having to entertain his mom and think of things to say...or rather, not say. I was seriously the worst conversationalist on the planet.

My brow furrowed as I watched him jump out and run around the front of his truck. Why was tonight so awkward? The other day at the hospital, I hadn't felt a bit uncomfortable. We'd talked and joked. But from the get-go tonight, I'd been on edge. Of course, having him pick me up at my apartment and be alone in his truck for so long felt more like a date than anything Riley and I had done.

I folded my arms. He should've brought his Barbie. Surely, she'd charm his mom. She'd certainly hoodwinked him.

Parker picked up a small woman and spun her in a circle. He set her on her feet and leaned in to kiss her cheek, then laughed and pulled a pencil out from over her ear. His mom covered her mouth and leaned over to laugh. She must've forgotten she'd put it there. I touched my heart at the tender smile Parker gave her. My brother would never have acted that way with our mom. Of course, my family hardly talked anymore. It was as if my parents considered their job done. They'd raised Mark and me to adulthood and now could actively pursue their careers without us in the way.

Parker wrapped an arm around his mom's waist and walked her to the truck. They appeared genuinely happy, not uptight and in a rush to push each other away, like how my parents acted with me and Mark.

Mrs. Harrington was short, like me, but she was graceful and willowy, whereas I had cursed curves. Her pixie cut brought out sculpted cheek-bones, and her clothes screamed comfort over fashion. Her bright disposition and energetic posture gave off a healthy, friendly vibe.

Parker threw her duffel bag into the bed of the pickup and opened the door. "Hey, Meridee." He grinned, casting a body-tingling spell over me as he pulled me from the truck. "This is my mom." He took my hand. "And this is my good friend, Meridee Mansford. You'll be staying at her place tonight."

His mother pulled me into a hug, and I stiffened. Never had I been hugged by a stranger.

"I'm thrilled to meet you, Meridee." She gave me an infectious smile I couldn't help returning. The same as her son's. "Parker's told me so much about you. Thanks for driving all the way up here to get me. I'm sure you had better things to do."

I blinked. Parker had told her about me?

Of course, he had. He would've had to say something about the girl she'd hang out with all weekend.

"I'm glad I could come," I lied.

He helped her into his truck, then turned to give me a hand up. The drive home passed much faster than the drive there had. Parker surged with life, whereas he'd seemed bored when it'd just been me in the truck with him.

No surprise there. You got what you paid for. If Parker ended up frustrated by my lack of people skills, he only had himself to blame.

He draped an arm over his mom's shoulders and asked about her flight, about nephews and nieces, and about how his sisters were doing. She beamed, and I could tell the woman adored her children. Parker's two older sisters and their children still lived with her. My mom would whip my hide if I did that. Even after my nightmare with Brody, she hadn't opened her home to me. I'd followed Mark up here to Washington to escape her disappointment.

Parker told his mom what he knew about me, which wasn't much. He said my major was exercise science. I didn't correct him. Everyone got it wrong and assumed I wanted to do fitness videos or be a high school gym teacher when I graduated.

"What did you do in high school?" his mom asked. "No." She put up a hand. "Let me guess." She grinned, and I couldn't help but laugh. She was so bubbly and friendly. So different than my own mom. "I bet you did Spanish or art club."

I gasped. "How did you know?" I'd taken four years of Spanish and could speak it fluently.

"Did you do both?"

"No. Just Spanish club."

She grinned. "I can picture you as a cute *senorita,* shaking some maracas."

Parker snorted, which made me glare at him.

"Watch the road, son." She elbowed him.

His head swiveled forward.

Mrs. Harrington kept asking questions. She had this serious *Star Trek* Borg thing going on where resistance was futile in keeping secrets.

"What brought you here? Do you live in state?"

"No. Well, I guess I do now." I squirmed. "My brother was attending school here, so after, uh..." My tongue rammed into the block wall of my past.

Mrs. Harrington rested her hand on mine. "After what, dear?"

"My divorce." Even after three years, I could barely say the word. "I had to get away, and Mark was here. So I joined him."

Parker leaned forward, his eyes practically bulging from their sockets. "You were married?"

His mom nudged him. "Keep your eyes on the road." She squeezed my hand. "I'm sorry."

"Don't be. I got what I deserved."

She clucked her tongue. "No one deserves heartbreak."

Oh, Brody had given me way more than that. I needed to change the subject. "Parker tells me you teach junior high."

"I do." She seemed to sense my need to stop talking and filled the awkward silence with a description of her students and other details about her career.

I nodded at the appropriate times, but what I really wanted to do was cry.

16

PARKER

*T*HOUGH IT'D BEEN an exhausting day, it'd also been an awesome one. I'd driven Mom around town, explored Military Hill, walked along the Palouse River, and showed her around campus—from the empty stadium to Ferdinand's, where Mare had treated us to ice cream. After Mare got off work, she'd made dinner for us at her place. Her lasagna had been divine. She certainly knew her way around a kitchen and would make some lucky guy super happy someday. But I didn't believe that guy would be Riley. They were two puzzle pieces that appeared like they should connect, but no matter how hard you tried to fit them together, they wouldn't lay flat.

After dinner, Mare had put in a DVD and we'd crashed on her couch. Two of her roommates returned and they'd begged me to sign several shirts and pillowcases. Mare had rolled her eyes and mouthed *Sorry,* but I was used to that kind of behavior from strangers.

Halfway through the movie, Mom stood and yawned. "I'm going to call it a night. I can't keep my eyes open anymore."

I paused the show. "It is an hour ahead for you."

"Do you need anything?" Meridee asked.

Mom pulled her into a hug. "I'm fine, dear. You've spoiled me. Finish watching the movie with Parker."

"Where's my hug?" I teased.

Mom opened her arms, and I wrapped her up in my embrace as she stood on her tiptoes to peck my cheek. "Love you, son. Thanks for an awesome day."

"Thanks for coming."

She disappeared into Mare's room.

I followed Mare into the kitchen.

"Do you want more popcorn?" she asked.

"You mean dessert of the gods?" The caramel popcorn she'd made earlier had sent me into rapturous bliss. "The answer is a resounding *Yes*." I winked. "Can't finish the movie without a heavenly treat and an angel beside me."

She placed a bowl of gooey popcorn in the microwave. "Well, one out of two isn't bad."

"You mean you won't make me popcorn?"

Her cheeks turned rosy as she shook her head at my teasing.

"Thanks again for dinner tonight. It was the best thing I've eaten in forever!"

"You're welcome."

"I can tell Mom enjoys your company. Thanks for hanging out with us today."

She fought back a smile. "She's so easy-going. I'm sure she enjoys everybody's company."

The microwave beeped. I stepped closer. "By the way, you look really nice tonight."

"Uh," she darted over to the fridge, "can you grab the popcorn?"

I chided myself for flirting. But she really did look hot. Her dark lashes framed bottomless brown pupils that teased, tempted, and enticed. Seriously. Her eyes, with just a hint of mascara, put Lily's to shame, and Lily spent big bucks on eyebrow stitching, permanent makeup, lash tinting, you name it.

"Sure thing." I grabbed the bowl of caramel yumminess and joined Mare on the brown sofa that'd seen better days. I tossed a handful of gooey popcorn in my mouth. "Can I hire you to be my personal chef?"

She grabbed the remote from the coffee table. "You couldn't afford my rates." She dimmed the lights and resumed our movie.

I leaned back into the cushions. But without Mom between us, I perceived details I hadn't earlier, like how scrumptious Meridee smelled when she shifted positions, and how tiny her hands were all clasped in her lap. Thoughts shifted into the danger zone as I recalled how delicate and soft her hand had been when I'd held it earlier.

I focused on the movie, shaking off my wayward thoughts. We laughed at the funny parts and groaned at some cheesy scenes. Being with Mare was so easy. No expectations. No pretending. No worrying I might say or do the wrong thing to upset her. I wished Lily could be chill like her.

Riley was lucky. Mare was super cool.

When the movie ended, I grabbed her hand. "Walk me to my truck."

She tugged her hand free. "But I'm warm and cozy in here."

"Come on, Mare. Please."

"It's Meridee."

I raised a brow. "I thought we already established that we're friends, and after today, we might even be buddies."

She laughed. "I don't know about that. You're a sucky friend, remember?"

"Sucky friend or not, I think I should be allowed to call you Mare."

She sighed. "Has anyone ever told you that you're a pain?"

I grinned. "Never. Everyone loves me. Including you. Now come outside with me."

She rolled her eyes, but marched to the door. Her roommates jumped up from the kitchen table as I followed her. They'd been not-so-subtly checking me out for the last half hour.

"Bye, Parker," the brunette called after me.

I waved, sending both of them into hysterical giggles.

That was another trait I appreciated about Mare. She didn't lose her head around me, which was refreshing.

I closed the door and followed Mare down a flight of stairs. As we approached my truck, I asked the question that'd nagged me since last night.

"Tell me about your marriage." She seemed way too young and sweet to have already been married and divorced. For her cooking alone, her husband should've kept her.

She wrinkled her nose. "It's a long story."

I opened my door. "I'm not in any rush. Get in. It's chilly."

She frowned but climbed onto the bench seat. I slid in beside her, shutting the door against the weather.

"I still can't get my head around the fact you've been married." She was so young.

Her knee started bouncing. "I was young and stupid."

"No one could ever call you stupid. Maybe naive."

Her lips twisted. "Yeah, that too."

"Were you high school sweethearts?" Maybe that's why she couldn't talk about it and why she hadn't dated for so long. The guy had broken her heart, and she still wasn't over him.

"Hardly." A myriad of emotions played across her face. I knew the moment she decided to spill. Her jaw clenched and her eyes focused beyond me. "Brody moved in the last semester of my senior year. I worked in the math lab and was assigned to tutor him so he could graduate."

"You must've been a sexy tutor."

"More like a gullible one." Her brows fused together. "Brody was every girl's dream. He made the rounds with the popular girls, as you'd expect, but as winter turned to spring and the end of school approached, he began flirting with me." She pinched her nose. "I should've known better, but I was so flattered by his attention that I lost myself."

Her shoulders drooped, making me angry for her sake.

"Mark hated Brody from the beginning and forbid me from hanging out with him. Said he was a major player." She shrugged. "That just made me mad and I went out of my way to spend more time with Brody." Her knee bounced harder. "Graduation night, Brody convinced me to drive to Vegas with him, instead of getting on the bus for the school-chaperoned Grad-Bash. He said we deserved to be together." She closed her eyes. "We drove six hours to Vegas and stopped at the first wedding chapel we found." She shuddered. "Half an hour later, after he'd stripped me of my virginity and pride, I found myself alone in a crummy motel room until the next night when Brody came crawling back, drunker than a skunk."

I wrapped an arm around her. "A-hole."

"The next morning he made me empty my savings. We moved into a dive in the barrio, and I never dared step outside. I have no clue what he did with all my money. I'd saved seventeen grand for college, and my parents had matched it. So I had thirty-four thousand dollars he burned through. That's all he'd wanted. Like an idiot, I'd bragged about how much I'd saved during one of our tutoring sessions. In hindsight, I realize that's when he started flirting. I should've known he wouldn't like me for any other reason."

"Are you kidding? You're amazing, Mare. What every guy wants in a woman."

She pushed my arm off her. "Says the guy with the perfect model girlfriend. You don't have to sugarcoat it, Parker. I know I'm not pretty, like Lily."

"Lily's only beautiful on the outside. You're the whole package. Looks, brains, kindness, and cooking. Any guy would be proud to claim you. I know Riley is."

She shook her head. "Why are you with Lily if you think so little of her?"

I fidgeted on the cracked, leather seat. I hadn't meant to badmouth Lil. "I don't know. I mean, she's gorgeous and I do like her." I just didn't like the games she played.

"Is that the only reason you're with her? Her looks?"

"No!" That made me sound so shallow. "She's a really nice girl. A leader. She's confident. Her family does a lot of good in the community." At least, their name seemed to be on everything from streets to the modern library. I frowned as I considered Lily's faults, which multiplied the longer I stayed with her. "I know she has some hang-ups, but everyone does." I did. "Why are you giving me the fifth degree anyway?"

"Because like you keep emphasizing, we're friends. I want you to be happy, and Lily didn't strike me as very nice when we met. Nor loyal."

I clenched my fists. "She has some trust issues. Her self-image is wrapped up in how others see her. I think that makes her act like a tease."

"And you're okay with that?"

"She's not flirting with other guys now that we're serious." At least, not that I knew.

"Are the two of you *serious*? Riley made it sound as though you're always at his place to avoid her."

Dang Riley and his big mouth. "I've avoided her recently just to get homework done and save money. She can be a little needy."

"Why don't you tell her your concerns?"

I scoffed. "That wouldn't go over well." Lily wouldn't settle. She expected all or nothing from her man. And sadly, I was close to having nothing left to give. I needed to do better. Make more time for her.

"A healthy relationship involves give and take, Parker. You shouldn't just be the giver."

"I'm not."

"Then why are you hiding? If she truly cares about you, she'll be sensitive to your needs. If you need more time to study, tell her. Or if you don't have lots of money, take her on a walk around the park or watch a Netflix movie."

That sounded marvelous, but Lily wasn't that type of girl. Mare was. I kind of envied her and Riley's relationship, even if it seemed a bit strained.

Lily and I had nothing like that. We had lust and passion off the charts, but the rest of our relationship hadn't moved out of the shallows.

"You don't understand."

"Then help me. Tell me what you see in her."

I scowled at the roof of my truck. "She's been my dream for two years. Two years! I've watched her with other guys and with a fiancé last year, and it killed me, because I knew we'd be perfect together. But she never even noticed me until this year."

"And you don't find that odd how she started paying attention after you became famous?"

"How do you know she wouldn't have picked me even if I hadn't shined this year? We really are perfect together. Everyone says so." I folded my arms. "I'd be a fool to throw away my dream."

She rested her hand on my arm. "Dreams can turn into nightmares. Brody taught me that."

I took a shaky breath. As much as I hated Mare probing into my personal life, I also appreciated it. Talking about things that mattered was liberating. I hadn't been able to talk about what had been bothering me forever. She really was a good friend.

"Your ex was a dang-blasted fool."

She made a face. "I better go. It's late."

I opened the door and helped her out. "Brody didn't deserve you, Mare. Really. You're way too amazing for a low-life like him."

Her expressive eyes bound me in place, touching me deep where I'd never explored. She swallowed. "You're too good for Lily. Find a girl who loves you for the fantastic guy you are beneath your fame and attention."

"Like you?"

She snorted as though I'd said something funny and surprised me by wrapping her arms around me. "Someone much better."

Her short hug made my body buzz as though I'd grabbed onto a live wire. I gulped, wishing I dared tell her I wasn't joking.

But that'd be wrong. She was my best friend's girl...and my friend.

"You really do deserve better than her." The way she gazed at me, those beguiling brown eyes caressing me, made me believe her.

"You might be right." Lily wasn't going to change. She was who she was. We'd never really meshed because of that. I couldn't tame her into the girl I wanted her to be, as much as I wished I could.

She ducked her head. "I'd better go. See you at the game tomorrow."

"Yeah."

I climbed in my truck and mulled over Mare's words. "*Find a girl who loves you for the fantastic guy you are beneath your fame and attention.*"

Mare was right. That wasn't Lily. I'd fought the truth for weeks but talking to Mare tonight had made everything clear. Lily only liked me *for* my fame and attention and only seemed interested in a physical relationship. She didn't seem to care about the guy I really was off the field.

I heaved a weary sigh. Problem was, the girl who saw the *real* me was totally unavailable.

17

MERIDEE

*M*Y FIRST FOOTBALL game overwhelmed me. So many people. Deafening noise. Rowdy fans. Rules I did not, and could not, understand. I'd been in a shell-shocked daze since Mrs. Harrington had led me inside the Stadium and located our seats midfield. Parker had asked me to come to support her, but the rambunctious fans and head-pounding noise intimidated me. Pam supported me instead, leaning over to explain each play and pat my arm in encouragement.

I didn't belong here.

The perfect Barbie dolls in their maroon and black tank tops, shaking their pom-poms and booties on the field below, were football-type girls.

Pam pointed. "Look! There's Parker."

In his helmet, pads, and white and red uniform, I never could've found him if she hadn't pointed him out. Seeing him in the hospital alone was much different than seeing him with a dozen other uniform-wielding giants. I tossed popcorn in my mouth, but kept my eyes glued to his number sixteen jersey. In his tight white pants, it was pleasurable work.

By halftime, I appreciated why Parker received the attention he did. His nickname, Sticky Fingers, had nothing to do with marshmallows over a fire or petty theft, and everything to do with how he never missed a catch. His nimble fingers latched onto the ball and held on as though made of super glue.

In the third quarter, Parker dived to catch another pass and two huge guys in blue and orange tackled him from behind. Others followed, and in a blink, I watched him disappear beneath a mountain of players. The referee blew his whistle to stop play, and I covered my mouth.

No way could Parker be uninjured.

When the ref reached him, Parker's hand raised with the ball clutched in his fingers. The pass was declared complete, and the crowd went berserk. I blew out a shaky breath, a little queasy and a lot angry that the show-off had elicited any sympathy from me.

"He almost gave me a heart attack."

Pam laughed. "I know, right? I lose years off my life every time he goes down. So many of his friends got injured during high school."

Parker jogged over to the lineup. When the ball snapped, he cut right, but couldn't ditch his defenders. Two more plays occurred before he caught a pass and made a first down. I still didn't understand what a first down was exactly, but Pam screamed and cheered whenever we got one.

The game stopped. Again. For the love of oatmeal, why couldn't they keep playing? It felt like there'd been at least fifty downs or stops. The tedious stopping and starting drove me bonkers. The game could've been over if they'd just keep playing.

Why did so many people love this sport?

I turned to Pam. "Parker's good. Does he plan on going pro?"

"He could. He loves the game and is talented enough, but it's only a tool to achieve his education. He values his body more than a multi-million-dollar contract. At least, I hope that's still the case."

I opened my mouth, but no words came out. She'd shocked me.

The Broncos gained possession of the ball on the next play. Parker and the rest of the offensive team jogged off the field.

I turned to Pam again. "Parker said his dad died. May I ask what happened?"

Her brows pulled together. "He hasn't told you?"

I shook my head.

"I'll leave that for him to share."

A lump formed in my throat. Pam had been so kind and open. The subject of her husband's death must be a sensitive one for her to avoid it.

She touched my arm. "It's my son's story. If he isn't ready, we should respect his wishes. Parker's had a difficult time dealing with his dad's death."

You'd never know it from watching the goofball. "He hides his pain well."

"You mean under his loud, obnoxious athlete mask?"

I grinned. "Exactly."

She stared across the field. "He's worn that mask since his dad died. He was super close to him but has blamed his dad for the hardships we've endured since. Deep down though, I believe Parker blames himself."

"Is there any way I can help?"

Pam wrapped an arm around me. "Just be his friend. You're good for my son. He has a sparkle in his eyes I haven't seen in years."

I gave her a shaky smile. More than likely, Barbie inspired his happy glow. I hoped he would be able to break her spell someday. He really did deserve someone better than that cheater.

Parker ran onto the field, and Pam and I stopped talking. I stared at the field but mulled over her cryptic clues. Her husband had died. Parker blamed himself for his death. Had his dad been in a car accident with him, and Parker survived? Or had his dad gone to pick him up from a friend's and died on the way there? What could cause a boy to feel responsible for someone's death?

The third quarter ended and the band began to play. Though Pam had been talking about Parker, I suddenly realized that I'd done the same thing. Blamed myself for circumstances beyond my control. Parker blamed himself for his father's death. But I'd blamed myself for what had happened with Brody. Maybe our choices had affected the outcome, but Parker had no control over life or death, and I couldn't control Brody's actions. But I certainly hadn't deserved what he'd done to me.

It was way past time to let go of my pain.

Tragedies had changed the course of our lives, but Parker and I could choose new paths. Happier ones. We didn't have to wallow in the past.

18

PARKER

*T*HE TRAINER APPLIED ice to my swelling ankle, making me wince. On the last play as I'd jumped to catch the ball, I'd been tackled from two different angles in the air before I'd hit the ground. When the referee had blown the whistle and declared a touchdown, number forty-three had climbed off my back and crushed his cleat into my ankle, making me miss the the last minute of the game.

By the time the trainer had finished treating my ankle, my teammates celebrated and high-fived each other in the locker room, reveling in the high that comes from a hard-earned victory. BSU usually kicked our trash, but we'd come off victors, thanks to that last touchdown. My bloody, sprained ankle was a small price to pay.

Jacob eyed my bandaged foot. "Number forty-three left you a nice parting gift, didn't he?"

"Oh, yeah."

Coach marched in and motioned to me. "The news crew wants a few comments. Keep them short and professional." I limped toward the exit. "I've sent Mike to bring your mom here so I can meet her," he said. "We'll be waiting for you in my office."

"Thanks, Coach."

The cameras surrounded me outside the tunnel, and Lily suddenly appeared. I bristled as she stroked my arm like I was a kitten. Meridee had pegged her right. Lily did bask in my fame. No matter how many times I told her to wait until my interviews ended, she always hijacked the camera's focus.

She pecked my cheek as the interviewer questioned me. He zoomed in on her staged performance, thrusting the microphone up to her lips.

"Are you Sticky Fingers' girlfriend?"

She caressed my jaw. "I am. Maybe even more soon."

I flinched. What was she talking about?

"Are there wedding bells in the future?"

I shoved in front of her. "No comment." I limped away. The interview was done.

"Wait up, Sticky." Lily caught me at the entrance and brushed my sweat-soaked hair. "You should've kissed me for the camera."

"They should stick to football questions. Why did you say *Maybe more*?"

She batted her eyelashes. "I want there to be more between us." She rubbed my lips. "I haven't seen you for the last two days."

"My mom's been in town."

"And you didn't introduce her to me?" She pouted.

A war took place inside me. Part of me wanted to break up with her this instant. Mare was right. I deserved better than being Lily's pawn in some messed-up game. Yet a stronger part wanted to prove we belonged together. I'd longed for this for years. To be cool. To be the guy everyone else wished to be.

"Sorry. I got busy."

"Too busy for me?" She pulled my head down and captured my lips.

And just like that, the battle was decided. I backed her up against the wall and deepened the kiss, desperate to prove I was man enough for her. That she couldn't live without me.

She tickled my chin. "When will you introduce me to your mom?"

I stared at her lips. "She's inside with Coach."

"Perfect." She walked two fingers up my chest. "I'll go change and meet you."

Not until she walked away did I groan. Lily was the last person I wanted Mom to meet. Curse her brain-freezing power.

I showered and dressed, chiding myself for the mess I'd made. If Mare saw me with Lil, she'd be disappointed. She wasn't a fan of Lil, and for some dumb reason, I cared about what she thought.

When I reached Coach's office, Mom flew across the room to wrap me in a hug. Meridee waved from a chair in the corner, and I wished I could hug her, too. She'd been the best this weekend, hanging out with Mom and me.

"What happened to your foot?" Mom asked. "I watched you limp off the field and have been worried sick about you."

"It's nothing, Mom."

Coach chuckled. "Mrs. Harrington, your son's one of the finest young men I've ever had the pleasure of coaching. He's a boon to the team, on and off the field. I wish I had twelve more of him."

Mom kissed my cheek. "Me, too."

When we left Coach's office, Riley met us and pulled Mare close. "Hey, Meridee." He pecked her cheek. "You picked a great game to come to for your first one."

"That's what everyone keeps telling me."

She seemed rather stiff, but that didn't mean much. Mare didn't like PDA.

"Meridee, can you introduce me to your young man?" Mom asked.

Mare turned bright red. "Uh, yeah. This is my friend, Riley Kirkpatrick. Riley, this is Parker's mom, Pam Harrington."

He reached out to shake hands. "It's wonderful to meet you, Mrs. Harrington. Your son's the best."

"He is, and since he picks good friends, you must be stellar as well."

He wrapped an arm around Meridee.

"Well," I said, "I know you're anxious to have your girlfriend back after I hogged her all weekend."

Riley gave Mare an adoring expression. "I *have* missed you."

"You know that dinner you owe me for getting Mare to a game?"

"Yeah, I'll—"

"Take her out, instead. She deserves it." I gave him a playful shove. "If you leave now, you might beat the crowds."

Meridee hugged Mom. "Bye, Pam. I'm so glad we could hang out."

"Thank you, dear. You've been a most gracious host...and friend."

I waved the lovebirds away, regretting that I couldn't thank Meridee properly. She'd saved me this weekend, and I'd had lots of fun with her. Maybe too much.

Time to get my head back in the game.

"Riley's nice," Mom said as I led her through the tunnel.

"Yeah."

"Meridee seemed uncomfortable with him though. And did you hear her introduction? She called him her friend."

I rolled my eyes. "He is her friend, Mom. Her *boy*friend."

"You seemed to light up whenever she was near."

I tugged at my collar. "She really is just my friend."

"But you like her, don't you?"

"Who doesn't like Meridee?"

"Parkie!" Lily approached, looking stunning in knee-length boots and a short skirt that revealed mile-long legs.

"Hey." I squirmed as she cuddled up to me.

"You must be Parker's mother." Lily stretched out a manicured hand.

"Yes, and you are?" Mom asked as she shook hands.

Lily stroked my arm. "I'm Parkie's girlfriend, and possibly more soon."

Mom's eyes widened. I wanted to crawl into a hole and die. Why did she keep saying that?

"I'm Lily Meyers. When he told me you've been here all weekend, I got upset that he didn't introduce us sooner. Boys!"

Mom pursed her lips. "Yes, boys. I'm sorry, but my son has never mentioned you before."

Thanks, Mom. I itched my neck and avoided Lily's glare. "I knew you were busy and didn't want you to feel obligated to hang out with us," I said.

"My son's so considerate." Sarcasm laced Mom's words.

Lily curled into my chest.

"Uh," I tried to unlatch myself from her. "I need to take Mom to the Spokane airport. You're welcome to join us, though it might be crowded in the truck." *Please say no*, I silently implored.

"I'd love to, but Jacob and the others are expecting me at the post-game party. When you return, join me. You're the star. Everyone will want to see you." As sweet as she sounded, I knew it wasn't a suggestion.

"Okay. See you in a few hours."

She planted her lips on mine and proceeded to give me a kiss that definitely wasn't fit for my mom to see. When she pulled away and winked, I cleared my throat and tugged at my collar.

"Goodbye, Mrs. Harrington. Nice to meet you. Next time we'll go shopping." She squealed and clapped. "I just know we're going to be besties. Ta ta."

"Not on your life, *chica*," Mom muttered as we headed to my truck.

She waited until we were seated inside the cab of my pickup before laying into me. "Your *girlfriend's* gorgeous."

"Yeah."

"I didn't even know you had a girlfriend. Why didn't you introduce her to me earlier?"

I shrugged.

"You wanted to hang out with Meridee, didn't you?"

I focused on the road. "I had no ulterior motives. I just knew Lily would make you uncomfortable."

"Why in tarnation are you with her then? That girl couldn't be more wrong for you if you tried. Have you two gone all the way?"

Not another interrogation. "No. But things are getting serious, so maybe soon. I'm an adult and can have sex if I want." I don't know why I lied. Maybe because she was treating me like I was still in high school. "She's beautiful and every guy wishes he was me."

"Except you."

"What's that supposed to mean?" Mom and I hardly ever argued, but when we did, watch out.

"You wish you were Riley."

I didn't respond. She'd hit too close to the truth, and it made me angry. But it didn't matter. If I broke up with Lily, I'd have no one. Right now, that sounded worse.

Sensing my foul mood, Mom changed the subject and didn't harp on me anymore. When we reached the terminal, I grabbed her duffel bag and helped her from the truck so she'd know she raised me right.

I squeezed her. "I love you."

"Love you more, Park. Sorry about getting all up into your craw."

"It's fine," I lied. "Thanks for coming to watch my game."

"I wish I could see every one of them."

I hugged her again, wishing the same thing. When she disappeared inside the terminal, I climbed back in my truck. The weekend had been way too short, and I wanted to kick myself for ending it on a sour note.

The drive back to Pullman gave me too much time to ponder. Coach had told me that two more NFL scouts had approached him last week. After my success on the field today, that number would rise. Was I being foolish not planning to enter the draft? Lily would think so. In fact, she'd be livid if I informed her of my intention. Maybe I should give it a try. One year playing pro wouldn't hurt, and I knew it'd make Lily ecstatic. Maybe enough to convince her that we belonged together. No more games. No more drama.

But as that idea marinated under the stars along that lonely piece of freeway, I wanted to puke. Playing pro had never been my dream. It'd been Dad's. Mom had supported my football career because I'd used it as a tool

96

to gain my education. I'd never imagined before this season that the NFL could be a possibility. But now, it was more than that. It was a given that I'd be a first-round pick and receive a huge contract.

My stomach kept churning as I reached Pullman and drove up College Hill. Judging by the cars lining both sides of the street, Carsen's party was still going strong even though it was after midnight. I parked at the end of the block and leaned my head against the steering wheel.

If I broke up with Lily, I'd be alone. Did I want that again? To be overlooked and invisible? I'd spent the first four years of college feeling like an intruder. A spectator. But being a part of Lily's inner circle had finally made me feel like I belonged.

But Mare wouldn't understand.

I punched the cracked vinyl seat.

Why should I care what Meridee thought? It's not like anything could happen between us. We were just friends. That's all.

Breaking up with Lily wouldn't solve my issues. It'd only leave me with too much time on my hands to think, and that was the last thing I needed right now.

I trudged toward Carsen's house, hoping a beer would settle my stomach.

Someone called out from the front porch. "Hey, Sticky Fingers is here."

I glanced up to see Tiny Mo blocking the doorway. "Hey, man."

Lily pushed him out of the way and grabbed my arm. "It's about time, Parkie. I've been lonely." She dragged me inside.

I high-fived Jacob and my other teammates and grabbed a beer as Lily led me to a couch in the shadows. She snuggled into my lap as I opened my beer and started chugging. When her lips found mine, I cast my nagging doubts about us aside.

No way would I cut her out of my life. That'd be stupid when she gave me everything I'd ever wanted.

19

MERIDEE

I'D ONLY BEEN to Riley's place once, when I'd brought over dinner that night he'd been sick. Beads of sweat rolled down my lower back as I climbed the flight of stairs to his apartment.

"Deep breath," I muttered. I was doing the right thing. It would hurt way less now than if I let things keep going.

I reached his door but couldn't bring myself to knock. Riley was super nice. The last thing I wanted to do was hurt him.

But maybe he'd be relieved. Even glad.

I was a super lame girlfriend.

But what if he got angry?

Bile rose up my throat. I winced and swallowed. *Just do it*, I told myself. *Riley's a good guy. He won't hurt you.* I willed my fist to lightly knock.

Footsteps from inside made my stomach churn. The door opened and Riley grinned.

"Hey! I wasn't expecting you." He pulled me into a bear hug.

I stiffened.

He relaxed his grip and motioned me inside. "Come in."

I followed him into his cramped, messy apartment.

"Is everything okay?" he asked.

"Let's sit." I dropped my gaze. Now, I wished I'd broken up with him after his last game. Instead, I'd stewed over my decision for days, before working up enough courage to come here.

Riley took a seat on the sofa, sitting further from me than usual. I peeked up at him and glimpsed pain gathering in his blue eyes.

He knew.

"Riley, I—"

Another guy came around the corner and stopped. "Oh, hey. I didn't know you had your girlfriend here." He gave me a chin tilt. "I'm heading to a job interview. Can I borrow your briefcase? To look more professional?"

"Sure." Riley sounded stiff.

"Can you help me find it, man?"

Oh, sweet Pete! Couldn't he sense the awkward vibes between us?

Riley's jaw ticked as he glanced at me. "Uh, I'll be right back, okay?"

And I'd be sprawled out dead on his couch from the suspense.

My head throbbed as I waited for Riley to find his briefcase for his procrastinating roommate. I already knew the case wouldn't help him. He had *flighty* written all over his face.

When Riley returned, he sat even further from me on the couch. "What did you come here to tell me?"

I sensed he already knew, going by the way his eyes stayed glued to his clenched hands. Taking a deep breath, I opened my mouth to speak.

Here went nothing.

FUMBLE & INTERCEPTION

20

MERIDEE

*F*RENCH VERBS SUCKED. I tapped my pen against the table, wishing I didn't have an oral exam in thirty minutes. It was pathetic that I had no problem memorizing anatomy terms or chemistry equations, but French verbs and words dangled just out of true understanding's reach. Why had I thought studying a third language was a good idea? I took a bite of my turkey-avocado sandwich and repeated verb conjugations under my breath.

I lifted my head to observe the cafeteria commotion. Green couches scattered about were punctuated by red tables and columns climbing to the ceiling. I smiled as I recalled how Parker had crashed into me right by the middle one. I'd wanted to fade into a puddle that day when the whole student body had focused their attention on us. Orange chicken, rice, and Doctor Pepper had covered me from head to toe, but not even a kernel of rice had stuck to Parker. His superior looks had made even a natural disaster quail and bow to him.

While I studied clusters of lingering students, the same man I'd been day-dreaming about appeared. Fans called out to him as he searched for a spot to sit. He paused at a couch with three coeds to sign autographs, before sliding into a seat not far away.

I automatically hunched behind my textbook, before chiding myself. What was I doing? I wanted to see Parker, not hide from him. Two weeks had passed since we'd hung out, and I hadn't run into him once. He hadn't even dropped by Ferdinand's for his bi-weekly cone.

I'd missed him.

I watched from behind my book, noting how his jaw tightened and relaxed as he chewed. Wow. He made even eating appear sexy. Watching him gave me peace about ending things with Riley. It'd been tough, but my feelings couldn't be denied. After my Brody nightmare, I hadn't believed it possible to ever trust again, but Riley had paved the way, and Parker had come in on his heels and dug his way into my heart until the weekend with his mother had sealed my feelings.

I really liked Parker Harrington.

I stood to go say hello, but sat down again as Parker waved at someone. Two huge football players I hadn't noticed and a couple of stunning cheerleaders joined him at his table.

I wrinkled my nose.

The goddess, Lily, snuggled right onto his lap. Her hair fell in perfect waves halfway down her back, and a braid fashioned over her head seemed to crown her queen. She ran her hand through Parker's dark hair, leaning in to claim him as her king.

Ick. I averted my gaze.

Clearly, he hadn't broken up with her. Why had I thought he would? Yes, he'd agreed with me that night that he deserved better. But even then, I'd known he hadn't been thinking about me. Lily was gorgeous, no denying that. And guys didn't seem to care about anything other than that.

Nails dug into my palms as Barbie baited Parker with fries. Her melodic giggle rang out whenever he nibbled them out of her fingers.

I guess it was cute. Romantic, even. But I wanted to march over and smack him upside his head. I'd thought he was better than other guys.

What a foolish fantasy.

I tried to focus on French verbs, but even my looming test couldn't stop me from stealing peeks at the perfect-looking couple. Parker laughed at everything she did and said. How dumb I'd been to entertain hope that a guy like him would care for me—even as a friend. Just because he'd held my hand and made me comfortable enough to reveal my secrets didn't mean he had feelings for me. Why would he when he had Beauty cuddled up on his lap? He'd be an idiot to trade her in for a freckled beast.

French verbs tasted like bile as I muttered them, not that they'd been very appetizing before. Maybe I should drop the stupid class. I'd never need French as an orthopedic PA and had no desire to visit Paris. All I wanted was to go home and bury myself in a tub of ice cream. Any flavor would do.

A gnawing headache began to form at the base of my skull as Parker kept stealing kisses from Barbie. I focused on my notes, but when he stood, I took note.

So did half of the students eating in the CUB.

Lily grabbed his wrist and batted her lashes, perhaps begging him to stay or kiss her goodbye.

He was probably eager to do both.

I recalled his declaration that he'd always known Lily would be perfect for him. And he was right. They made a stunning couple. Parker settled his lips on hers, and I turned away.

When I looked back, Parker swung his backpack over his shoulder and took off with one last wave to his princess.

Seconds after he disappeared, Lily draped her arm around the Thor double, who made a crude gesture in the direction Parker had gone, before pulling her onto his lap and proceeding to kiss her far more passionately than Parker had.

I choked on a bite of sandwich as I watched them maul each other. Digging out my phone, I began to record the scene to clue Parker into her deceit. This time I'd have proof. He'd have to listen.

But when the sickening couple took off together, I set my phone down and shook my head.

What did it matter?

When women possessed such devastating beauty as Lily, their faults didn't matter to guys. Or their loyalty, I guess. It's not as though Parker would break up with her and want to give his heart to me if I showed him proof of her cheating. I'd just make him feel bad as I popped his imaginary bubble.

Nothing could be gained by badmouthing Barbie. Parker didn't care for me, even as a friend, as his avoidance of me implied. Why would he? I was plain, boring Mare, and would always be invisible to guys like Parker Harrington.

21

PARKER

THIRTY THOUSAND FEET up in the air, I clenched my jaw as Lily headed down the narrow aisle. Why couldn't she leave me alone? We were done. Finished. I refused to be played again after what I'd witnessed the other night. I regretted being played twice because I'd refused to listen to Meridee or my gut.

Instead, I'd wasted the last three weeks jumping through hoops to prove to Lily that I was her perfect man. I'd gone apartment hunting with her, even though I knew Mom would freak if she found out. I'd agreed to enter the draft after she had a melt-down about my original intentions. I'd let my studies slide to prove my devotion. And what had she done but throw it all back in my face and make me the laughingstock of the team.

Lily was a flirt. A tease. We'd never connected on any emotional, intellectual, or spiritual level because she only loved herself. I'd just been too blinded by her physical traits to see that or believe the truth when Mare had pointed it out.

The team was flying to Los Angeles to play USC. I'd sought a place in the rear of the plane with the married guys and some of the calmer single players like Riley so I could catch up on homework. Lily and her crowd usually hung out near the front. I hadn't wanted to talk to them. Lily had painted me as the inexperienced fool for them to mock.

She went to slide into the empty seat next to me, but I shook my head. "Riley's sitting there," I lied. His seat was two rows up and he was in the john at the moment.

Lily scooted in anyway.

I blocked her with my backpack. "I have nothing to say to you. Go keep Carsen happy up front."

She shoved my bag onto the floor. "You pushed me to him, you know?" She dabbed at her eyes. "I never felt like you wanted me."

I scowled. "So your cheating is my fault?"

She touched my hand. "Carsen craves me. You just crave your books. I won't be anyone's seconds."

I scoffed. What a piece of work. Even though she'd cheated on me, she truly saw herself as the victim. "After what I witnessed the other night, I'll stick to my books. They're not cheap and trashy."

Her eyes narrowed into slits, but I doubted she felt an ounce of regret. Lily thought too highly of herself to admit she'd done wrong.

It shouldn't have surprised me to find her and Carsen together. The signs had been there all along. I'd just chosen to ignore them.

But no more. I could see now that my whole relationship with Lily had been toxic.

As a boy, I'd owned a black lab named Revit. Mom had warned me to never give him chocolate, grapes, or raisins. Those were toxic to dogs. But whenever I ate a candy bar, Revit would give me his sad puppy-dog eyes and make me feel like a jerk for not sharing. The day after my ninth birthday, Revit had given me those woeful eyes as I ate leftover chocolate cake. I'd wanted him to know I loved him best, so I'd convinced myself that chocolate cake wasn't the same as a bar of chocolate. It was bread, and Revit loved bread. I'd scooped up a generous helping and let him eat it from my hands. His tail had wagged harder and happier than I'd ever seen, and he'd licked my hands in gratitude as I gave him a second piece.

But an hour later, I'd found my best friend dead on my bedroom rug. My kindness had killed him.

Now, I was Revit, and Lily that tempting chocolate cake.

For two years, I'd craved her and whined to God to give us a chance because I'd believed we would be perfect together. But she hadn't been good for me. I'd sensed it deep down as I'd worried about our shallow relationship, but I'd brushed it aside as something that would fix itself over time. I'd battled doubts whenever Lily had said hurtful things to others, and I'd especially wondered about us as she'd kept trying to seduce me, even after I'd explained that I wouldn't have sex until we were more committed. But like a dumb dog salivating over chocolate, I'd been too blind to see the truth.

My eyes were opened now though. I couldn't change who Lily was, and I didn't like the person she chose to be.

She caressed my cheek. "I love you, Park, but I need more from you. Come to my hotel room tonight." She blew into my ear, but I felt nothing.

"Go to hell...or Carsen. Whichever one will take you."

She pouted. "I won't give you another chance."

"Is that a promise?"

She stood and scowled down at me. "We're done. I'm sick of your attitude."

"Thank you, God," I muttered as she stormed back up the aisle.

I grabbed Riley's arm when he walked by. "I saved you a seat, man."

He gave me a wary expression as I moved my bag out of the way.

Wade Turner, a married guy sitting across the aisle, snorted. "Sticky Fingers ticked off the gorgeous Miss Meyers and needs protection."

Riley raised an eyebrow.

I shrugged. "She did come by. I told her you were sitting here."

Riley grunted. "Smart man." He rubbed the back of his neck.

My fingers curled and stretched as I wondered how to apologize for ditching him the last few weeks. "Look, Ry. I'm sorry for ignoring you." I kept my voice low, not wanting Wade or anyone else to overhear. "I've been trying to figure out life and..." I shook my head. "I only screwed it up more."

His brows pulled together. "Please tell me the rumor that you're shacking up with Lily isn't true."

I grimaced. "You couldn't pay me enough to live with that two-timing tease."

Riley tapped his fingers together. "Did you break up with her?"

I puffed out my cheeks. "Yeah, and after catching her with Carsen the other night, there's no way in hell I want her back."

"Good. I never could stand the brainless git."

I laughed. "I've missed you, man."

"Of course, you have."

We began bantering back and forth, and I basked in our easy camaraderie. I'd been a fool to let our friendship slide.

"Let's hang out when we get home," he said as we taxied onto the runway at LAX.

"I'd love that." It would mean seeing Meridee again, and that would be a punch to my heart, but ignoring him hadn't brought positive results. I'd rather deal with the pain of seeing Mare and him together than not see my friend at all.

22

PARKER

*G*AZING INTO THE mirror, I winked and put both thumbs in the air, like the Fonz. I sighed and shook my head. It didn't matter how cool I appeared or acted tonight, I'd never win Mare's heart. And that was as it should be. She was Ry's. And he deserved someone awesome.

Still, I took extra care preparing for my date.

After the USC game last weekend, I'd avoided Lily and her cronies and had camped out at Riley's. We'd stayed up late playing X-box and had fallen back into comfortable patterns. But tonight's double-date had me ready to hurl. I wanted to be happy for my friend, but I knew it'd be torture to see him and Mare together. They'd had a whole month to grow closer. Maybe their puzzle pieces fit now.

I dabbed on cologne and left to pick up the blind date Riley had set me up with. Some chick named Jennifer. An accounting major. I crossed my fingers that the night wouldn't be a total disaster.

I found the girl's apartment and knocked. Maybe I should've brought flowers to appear excited, though that'd be a big, fat lie. I dreaded this evening.

A tall brunette opened the door.

"Are you Jennifer?"

"I am. And you're Parker. You don't have to introduce yourself to me. I'm your biggest fan."

Great. Riley had set me up with a groupie.

As I drove across town to the Birch and Barley, Jennifer gave me a rundown of every one of my games and even suggested strategies I should implement in the next game against Oregon. I tuned her out and focused on the road.

Why couldn't Riley have set me up with a quiet date?

My stomach churned as I led Jennifer into the restaurant. This was the moment I'd see Mare again. Hopefully, I kept my emotions under wraps.

Riley greeted us in the lobby. Alone. But then an olive-skinned girl with ebony hair joined him, taking his hand. Ry gave her an adoring smile, making my jaw drop.

What was going on?

Where was Mare?

The rest of the evening was a wash for my poor date. I didn't mean to ignore her but was too enthralled with Riley and his Hispanic princess to pay attention to Jennifer. Besides, if I wanted coaching advice, I'd listen to Coach Mike, not an accounting major.

Riley seemed smitten with Marcella—his exotic date that wasn't Meridee—and I couldn't be more thrilled that the girl on his arm wasn't the one I'd been agonizing over for the last month. Curiosity killed me as we ate dinner and went bowling. I yearned to know what had happened to Mare. Questions piled up inside me, making me the worst date ever.

Riley called me out on it after we dropped off our dates. "What was with you tonight, man? You hardly said two words to Jennifer. I could tell she was put off by your attitude."

"What's up with you?" I retorted. "I assumed you were with Meridee, and you show up with Zorro's chick on your arm, instead."

Riley snorted. "You really have been out of it. Meridee broke up with me right after the BSU game. You might've known that if you hadn't ignored me all month."

I bowed my head. "Sorry."

"Don't be. I know you had your plate full with Lily."

"So, what happened with Mare?" I clenched my hands in my lap.

He shrugged. "She told me she respected me and had enjoyed our time together. I'd restored her faith in men, but she didn't want to lead me on. She only liked me as a friend."

"Ah." I sighed. "The F-word."

"Yeah, but I can't be mad. She was super sweet about the whole thing."

His words twisted my gut. Even if Mare was unattached, what kind of putz would I be to go after her while my best friend still pined after her? That went against the bro-code.

Riley grabbed hot chocolate from the pantry to make a cup of Moe. That's what he called his caffeine-free drink of choice. "Want some?"

"If you're offering." I cracked my knuckles. Hope had lifted my spirits, but Riley's words had dashed them to pieces again.

He brought two steaming mugs over. I sat across from him, turning my mug around in my hands.

"So, you miss Meridee?"

He shook his head. "At first, yeah. But since I crashed into Marcella's cart at Walmart, I've hardly given Meridee a second thought. Marcella's incredible."

"Really?"

He sipped his cocoa. "Yeah. It was love at first sight. For both of us. Marcella's so easy to talk to, so warm and welcoming. And she's gorgeous! You should see her dance." He sighed. "I know it's too soon to say this, but I think I'm in love."

Hope flickered to life again. He'd never said so many sappy things about Mare. "You don't have any lingering feelings for Mare?"

Riley's mouth slowly twisted into a smile. "You've been crushing on Meridee, haven't you?"

I chewed my bottom lip, unwilling to confess my crime.

He chuckled. "You have! Is that why you stopped hanging out with me?"

I winced. "I didn't mean to fall for your girl, but after spending the weekend with her and my mom, I couldn't bear watching you two together anymore. I was jealous of your easy relationship."

Riley took another long sip of cocoa. "All this time I assumed you didn't consider me cool enough to hang out with, but you were just being the better man."

I shook my head. "That's impossible. You're the best guy I know."

We focused on our steamy mugs.

"I'm not with Meridee anymore," Riley said, "nor do I have any feelings for her now that I've met Marcella. I wouldn't think less of you if you went after her. In fact, I think you should."

A grin erupted all over my face. "I suddenly have a hankering for huckleberry ice cream."

Riley laughed. "Go get her, cowboy."

23

MERIDEE

CARAMEL SYRUP DRIPS were the bane of my existence. At Ferdinand's, at least. The hospital had much worse banes not fit to discuss in company. Sean joined me as I scrubbed sticky sap off the front of the counter.

"Ah, car-a-mel, my sweet love," he said in an exotic accent.

I bit down on my lips, fighting a smile. Mr. Owens might want me to be friendlier, but managers couldn't afford to be friends. Especially to flirts like Sean. But I appreciated his wit. His sarcastic barbs and cheesy pick-up lines made my shift fly by faster. He'd only started two weeks ago but had proved to be an efficient employee.

The bells jingled after I sent him into the back to grab refill tubs of ice cream. I put on a smile but froze as Parker Harrington strutted through the door.

"Meridee!" A huge grin appeared on his handsome face.

An icy boulder dropped into the pit of my stomach. What was he doing here? I'd done so well this past week not thinking about him. And now he'd gone and blown it all to Mars.

I grabbed a rag and squeezed. "If it isn't Sticky Fingers. Where's your fan club? I didn't imagine you capable of walking without two or three adoring fans propping you up."

"Ha ha. You're a riot."

I pulled back my shoulders. "What flavor brings you in today?" I would play it cool. Act as if nothing had happened between us. Because nothing had, or ever would.

"You."

I scrubbed the shiny counter as Sean emerged from the back. He glanced up and straightened.

"Hey, you're Parker Harrington."

Parker grinned and nodded.

"Yes," I said, rolling my eyes, "this is the all-mighty Sticky Fingers. Why don't you take his order so I can do inventory in the back." I whipped around and fled through the swinging door.

Alone in the back room, I leaned against the wall. Why had he come? It'd been over a month since I'd seen him. I'd chalked him up to a casualty of venomous Barbie.

I grabbed a clipboard and pencil. It wasn't Parker's fault I'd fallen for him. He oozed charm and sex appeal that made every girl worship him. But my attraction had become dangerous. That's why I needed to avoid him. He wasn't just a sexy body to fantasize about anymore. I'd grown to really like the man beneath all that hunk-a-licious muscle—the one who adored his mother and wasn't embarrassed to hug or kiss her in public, the one who'd played with sick children and made them smile, the one who had seemed to see and like the real me. For a moment. But I couldn't be his friend and watch him be used up by a woman I despised, a woman who was so wrong for him.

I began counting inventory, forcing Parker from my mind. But Sean poked his head around the door.

"Hey, there's a long line. Can you help a newbie?"

I wrinkled my nose. "Sure."

Dang. Duty called.

Donning my apron, I returned to the cash register. A quick perusal of the shop showed Parker sitting at a corner table eating his usual triple decker waffle cone. For a second, my heart constricted as I realized I hadn't made it for him. I'd always filled his order, and with great care.

But this was for the best. I needed to keep my distance from that man.

When the crowd of customers dissipated, I slipped into the back again. My nerves were fried from seeing Parker. I realized more than ever how foolish I'd been to raise my hopes to his level.

Sean found me again. "Harrington asked me to tell you to stop hiding and come face him like a man." He snorted. "His words, not mine. Are you two friends?"

I buried my head in my hands. "Tell him I've left for the night. I'll clock out and drive around the block until I see him leave. Can you handle things on your own for ten minutes?"

"Sure." His eyes crinkled. "You're probably the only girl on campus who'd run away from the big football hero, instead of jumping into his lap, you know."

"It's complicated."

He laughed. "Get out of here."

"I owe you."

"How about giving me next Saturday off."

"Deal." I'd cover his shift myself if needs be.

I slipped out the delivery entrance and drove around campus. When I returned and saw no sign of Parker's truck, I parked in the rear and berated myself for being dumb. What had my life come to that I had to hide from the big man on campus?

I entered the shop from the back and peeked up front. "Is the coast clear?"

Sean smirked. "Yeah. Harrington acted put-out that you left without saying goodbye, but he got over it. We talked about last week's game, and he's super chill. That surprised me since he's so famous." He grabbed a rag. "So why did you run?"

I frowned. "He ran me over in the CUB a few months ago and covered me in orange chicken. Whenever I see him, something awful happens."

Sean waggled his brows. "I think he *likes* you, Meridee. You should've seen his face when you walked away from him. He looked like you'd stolen the last cookie from the cookie jar."

"Yeah, right." I began buffing the stainless steel counter. Guys never did a thorough job. "You obviously haven't met his girlfriend."

"He has a girlfriend?"

"Yeah." I threw my rag down and grabbed a box of sugar cones from below the counter. "And she could win a Miss Universe pageant. No joke. Parker would never be interested in a girl like me."

"Why not?" He took the empty box from me. "You're cute."

I scowled and considered swatting him with my soiled rag. Why did guys consider that a complement?

"You are. Take it from a guy with eyes." He waggled his brows. "Those pageant princesses are nice to look at and maybe have a short fling with, but they're too spoiled and high-maintenance to endure long-term. I dated one in high school, and believe me, she wasn't worth the trouble. Guys like cute girls way more than pampered princesses. You're way more fun to cuddle because you're not all prickly."

"Yeah right." I refilled the caramel container.

Sean was only buttering me up because he wanted time off next weekend. He'd say whatever it took to flatter me. But I knew the truth. Guys like Parker Harrington didn't appreciate girls like me. Cute garnered chin pinches and friendships, but not serious relationships.

24

PARKER

*S*HADOWS HID ME as I staked out the street. For the past three days, Mare had successfully avoided me. Her coworkers had claimed she wasn't working, but I'd spotted her car in the back. When I'd pointed that out, the new guy had said her car needed to be towed. The next day, her car disappeared as well.

I couldn't figure out what had turned her against me. I had thought we'd become good friends after that weekend with my mom and had hoped we could become more now that Riley had withdrawn from the picture.

But luck was on my side today. Earlier, when I'd left the creamery disappointed again, I'd driven aimlessly around campus and had stumbled upon Mare's blue Corolla parked in an empty lot near the Ag building. I'd pulled up next to it and had recognized the two *Despicable Me* minion bobbleheads on her dashboard. She must've parked out here so I wouldn't see her car at Ferdinand's.

Knowledge was power.

Since she refused to see me when I'd come to her, I decided to wait for her to come to me. Shielding my phone, I checked the time. Ferdinand's had closed half an hour ago. Mare should appear any minute. When I heard footsteps, I rubbed my hands together.

A lone shadow appeared on the other side of the street. She checked both ways before crossing and made her way over to the dark lot.

I shook my head. When I got a hold of her, I'd give her a good talking-to for parking out this far at night. It wasn't safe.

Meridee jerked to a stop and inhaled sharply.

I covered my mouth, knowing she'd detected my handiwork.

"What the..." She stepped closer.

My cheeks hurt from stifling laughter. I'd done a bang-up job spelling *Got Ya* across her windshield in Oreos.

As Meridee circled her car, I stepped out from behind the bush. "Boo!"

She flipped around and shrieked, making me erupt in laughter.

"P-Parker?" she stammered.

"Yeah." I stepped closer. "Found you."

She smacked my chest. When I snickered, she kicked my shin.

"Ow!" I cried.

"You almost gave me a heart attack. What were you thinking scaring me like that?"

"Whoa, girl." I took hold of her arm. "I didn't mean to frighten you. I just wanted to surprise you." I glanced around the lot. "Although this lot is freaky scary. What were you thinking parking out here? What if I'd been a bad guy?"

"Who says you aren't?" She shook my hand off her arm. "You've been stalking me for days, sending annoying texts, and now have defaced my windshield."

I grinned. Anger looked mighty sexy on her.

She backed up against her filthy Corolla when I took a step closer. I reached around her to grab a cookie off the windshield.

"I didn't deface your property." I popped the Oreo in my mouth. "These are the good ones. Double Stuff." I pulled another one off and held it out to her.

She flung her cookie across the parking lot. "Gross. I haven't washed my car in forever. Who knows what's on that."

I peeled another Oreo off the glass to eat. "Grime adds flavor."

She scowled. "Why are you here?"

"I've been trying like crazy to see you."

She unlocked her door with jerky motions. "Well, you've seen me. Now go."

I grabbed the door so she couldn't close it. "I also wanted to talk to you."

She clenched the steering wheel. "You've blabbed plenty. Can you just go already?"

"Riley dropped me off. I'm sort of stranded here."

Her lips pressed into a firm line. "You have two strong legs."

I clutched my heart. "You'd leave me alone to walk home in the dark and get eaten by vampires or werewolves? Where's your heart, girl?"

She rolled her eyes. "I don't have one."

I stuck my lips out and pouted.

She huffed. "Oh, all right. Get in, you big baby."

I hurried over to the passenger side.

When she pulled away, she squinted. "Your cookie mess makes it hard to see."

"Be glad I didn't plaster the whole thing." I'd considered it but had run out of Oreos.

She shook her head, but I caught a hint of a smile. When she pulled in front of my building, I spotted Carsen and Jacob out on my balcony. Lily had probably sent them over to sway me. She'd texted all week to let her come over and talk.

Not happening.

"Uh, would you mind taking me to Riley's?"

Her brow furrowed, but she didn't question me as she pulled away and backtracked. When we parked in front of Riley's ancient complex, I reached for her hand.

"Thanks, Mare."

"You're welcome." She wiggled her fingers free.

"Have I upset you?"

She shook her head.

"Why have you avoided me then?"

She pinched her neck. "I don't know."

"Are we still friends?"

She squirmed but wouldn't meet my gaze. "I guess."

"Then I need to work on making you say *Yes. Absolutely.*" I leaned over the gear shift to plant a kiss on her cute, freckled cheek. "Night, Mare." I started laughing. "That didn't sound right. I guess when I say goodnight, I might call you Meridee."

"Nightmare is probably more accurate."

"No way. When I think of you, I only have sweet dreams."

She smacked my arm. "Don't be a dweeb."

I hopped out and waved.

We'd made progress tonight, but I didn't dare push further. She might run and hide again.

With things how they stood, she still might.

25

MERIDEE

_S_OMETHING HIT ME. "Get up. You have to see this." My roommate pulled the covers off my bed.

I rolled over and groaned. "What time is it?"

"Who cares? Come out. Hurry up." She bounced up and down in her Seahawks sweatshirt.

I swung my legs over the side and rubbed my eyes. "What's going on?"

"Just come outside. You'll never believe it."

I doubted I'd care. _Imagine Dragons_ could be doing a concert out on the lawn, and I'd skip listening to my favorite band to get one more hour of sleep. But my insistent roommate grabbed my arm and dragged me onto our balcony.

I blinked. And blinked again. What I saw stunned me even more than an impromptu rock concert.

Parker Harrington stood on the raised grassy area outside my apartment building, washing my car. I gaped at the scene, my sleep-deprived brain attempting to figure out how he'd moved my Corolla from its parking spot to the grassy heights. He didn't have my keys, and even if he did, he couldn't have driven a car up the narrow stairway to get it up the three feet of height separating the lawn from the sidewalk.

"What are you doing?" I yelled down to him.

"What does it look like?" He raised the hose and shot a stream of water up at me.

I squealed and jerked to the side as water splashed the spot where I'd stood. I glanced down, just now realizing I wore only my sheer pink lamb pajama top and shorts. I yelped and ducked inside to change into leggings and a sweatshirt. I pulled my tangled hair into a messy ponytail and bumped into my roommate as I exited.

"That's Parker Harrington." She grabbed my arm. "I almost passed out when he knocked on our door."

Dang Parker. I marched downstairs and approached with hands on hips.

He lifted his head and gave me a once-over. "Well, hello, beautiful. Why did you change? The sheep pajamas were smoking hot."

"Are you trying to get me in trouble? You can't bring my car up here. And why are you washing it in this freezing weather anyway?"

"You want me to wash you instead?"

A stream of water hit my face, making me scream and sputter.

Parker hooted.

I leapt forward and yanked the hose from his hands. "You find that funny?" I raised the nozzle.

He ducked behind the trunk of my car. "Now, Mare, don't do anything rash. If you start a water fight, I promise you'll lose."

I squeezed the nozzle, sending a breath-catching stream of water over the trunk. When he yelped, I kept the water pointed on that sweet spot.

"You are so going to pay." Parker jumped up and sprinted toward me with shocking speed.

I shrieked and tried to stop him with a blast of water, but he tackled me and wrestled the hose from my hands. Turning the nozzle, he let me feel its full force. I dropped to my knees, laughing and begging for mercy.

"I warned you not to start a water fight with me."

A brisk breeze rustled bare branches. I shivered and twisted my sweatshirt to wring water from it. "I'll remember that when you decide to wash my car again." I pointed to my sparkling Corolla. "How in the world did you get it up here?"

"It wasn't easy. But offer ten football players a few dozen donuts and they can accomplish anything."

I hugged myself. "How will you get it down?"

He waggled his brows. "Riley's bringing them back in a few minutes."

"You didn't need to do this." I couldn't believe he'd washed my car. It probably hadn't met with soap and water since last spring.

"Oh, I really did need to soak you." He chuckled. "You needed to be taught a lesson, although I must admit, I'm impressed by your aim."

He sauntered over to a tree and retrieved a Ziploc bag that held Oreos he'd peeled off my windshield. He opened the bag and stuffed a cookie in his mouth.

"Give me that." I ripped the bag from his hands. "You're going to kill yourself eating those."

"But they're delicious," he said through a mouthful of cookie.

I wrung my hands. "I hope you don't get me in trouble with this stunt. Cars aren't supposed to be up here."

"Chill, Mare."

Loud yelling and cat-calls made me turn. Parker's truck pulled into view, filled to overflowing with massive football players. When it parked in a handicapped spot by the stairs, Riley jumped out and waved.

"Morning, Meridee."

I lifted my hand as the muscular jocks hopped out of the bed of the truck and onto the ledge. Surrounding my puny car, the massive Polynesian called Tiny Mo counted off, and they lifted my Corolla in unison and carried it over to the ledge, where they worked to lower it and move it to an open parking space with seeming ease.

"Hey, Mare." Parker pinched my chin. "Do me a favor and don't hide when I come by Ferdinand's tonight."

I frowned. "Why do you want to see me?"

"Don't you know?"

I shook my head.

He gave me one of his heart-melting smiles, and I couldn't help but return it. I'd missed seeing him, though I needed to remember that he didn't care about me. He was just being nice.

"No one else can scoop my ice cream as perfect as you do."

"You're a nut."

"Nuts about you."

Riley honked.

"Gotta go." Parker winked. "But I'll see you tonight." He jogged over to his truck and hopped in the passenger door. Sticking his head out the open window, he yelled, "Don't park under those trees by the Ag building. I don't want a bird ruining my hard work."

I laughed. After his truck disappeared, I pinched my arm to double check I was awake. The last twenty minutes had felt very much like a dream.

26

PARKER

*W*IND HOWLED AND blew snow sideways. The first storm of the season. Good thing it had waited until tonight and not this morning when I'd washed Mare's car. I grinned as I recalled her startled expression when she'd walked out onto her balcony and spotted me. So worth the effort it'd taken to move her car up on the lawn and wash it for her. Especially seeing her in those sexy lamb pajamas before she'd changed. Talk about hot.

I hopped out of my truck and waved to Riley as he pulled away from Ferdinand's. The storm was worsening. I pulled a knit hat over my head and spotted Meridee near the front door, locking up. Practice had gone late since we'd had to watch reels for the upcoming game. I ran through drifting snow and smashed my face against the glass.

She yelped and jumped back, not having seen me approach in the dark.

"Can you let me in? It's freezing out here."

She scowled but unlocked the door.

I rubbed my hands together and stomped snow off my boots. "Thanks. You're a lifesaver."

"What are you doing out in this storm? Are you here to steal more tubs of expired ice cream?"

"No, I'm here to steal you once you're done. I'll help clean up and catch a ride home with you, if you don't mind."

She narrowed her eyes. "What if I do mind?"

I shrugged. "Riley dropped me off. His car's in the shop, so I told him he could use my truck for a date if he brought me here."

"Because it's so fun to mop floors and wash sticky tables?" She watched me closely.

"Well, yeah. Anything's fun with you."

She headed through the back door. I paced in front of the cash register until she returned with a rolling bucket of soapy water and a mop sticking out the side. She handed me the mop.

"You can clean floors while Danny and I work in the back." She put her hands on her hips, as though expecting me to argue.

"Yes, ma'am." I saluted and pushed the bucket of sudsy water into the far corner.

For the next twenty minutes, I mopped every square inch of tile. After I finished, Meridee showed me where to dump my mucky water and hang the mop. She turned off lights and grabbed her coat.

"Bye, Danny." She waved as her coworker pushed out the back door. She locked up and set the alarm. "Come on," she said to me over her shoulder.

Huge flakes of snow and gusts of wind made it difficult to see across the lot. I grabbed her hand and pulled her through the snow that'd already built up on the roads. It took several tries before she succeeded in getting her gutless engine to turn over and start.

We drove away, and I asked, "Want to watch a movie?"

She shook her head. "This storm's getting worse. I'm taking you to your apartment and getting off these roads."

"Fair enough. Take me to Riley's though."

Her lips pursed. "I hope you don't pay rent on your place."

"I'm trying to sell my contract and get into Riley's complex."

"Oh. Good luck."

The snow-packed streets made the few minute trip across campus take fifteen. I didn't complain. More time with Mare.

"Will you be okay driving home?" I asked, noticing the skin on her knuckles stretched taut over the steering wheel. "I can drive you if you want and text Riley to pick me up after his date." I wanted to spend more time with her.

"Don't worry about me. I'll be fine."

"That's a given. Will you promise not to hide tomorrow when I come in for some huckleberry heaven? I'd like to take a walk with you on your break."

"In this weather?"

I nodded. "Dress warm."

"Why?"

"Because dressing warm will keep you—"

"No. I mean, why can't you tell me whatever it is now?"

"There's nothing specific." I raised my eyebrows. "I just want to walk. Get to know you better."

Her brows pulled together. "Why?"

I tapped her nose. "Stop asking questions like a two-year-old. And don't hide from me anymore. I've missed your adorable face out front."

"Okay?" She sounded confused, which made me smile as I hopped out and waved.

"See ya tomorrow, Mare."

"Uh...yeah."

I jogged up the stairs through swirling snow. When I peeked over my shoulder, she still sat in her car watching me with a bewildered expression.

27

MERIDEE

Y STOMACH MIMICKED a Mentos mint in a bottle of Coke as I studied my reflection in the break room mirror. I'd ditched my hat and had applied a light shade of lipstick. But did I honestly believe Parker Harrington would care? Women who looked like models chased after him. No amount of makeup or fancy clothes would change who I was. Parker only came in for his bi-weekly dose of ice cream. And he happened to be social. That's all.

I returned to the front to find him waiting for me. His heart-melting smile appeared, causing my stomach to bubble even more. Maybe I'd get sick and have to cut this encounter short.

"Hey, Mare. I wondered if you were hiding."

"Nope, I was, uh...cleaning the supply room."

"Can you take a break?" He waggled his eyebrows.

I chewed my lip, wondering why he wanted to hang out with me. It made no sense. "Yeah. Sure." I turned to Tara. "I'm taking my break. Be back in ten."

"Or twenty," Parker added.

I folded my arms. "Ten."

He ducked under the red canvas line holder. "Fine. But don't start counting until you're bundled up and we're outside."

I returned to the break room to grab coat, gloves, and hat. Parker took my hand and pulled me out the door.

"Uh," I tried to extract my fingers. It wouldn't do his playboy reputation any good to be seen with a nobody like me.

He tightened his grip.

"What are you doing?" I asked.

"It's icy. Don't want you to slip."

Arctic air seized my throat, making my whole body shiver. "It's freezing out here. Let's sit inside." Then he wouldn't have to hold my hand to keep me on my feet.

"No way. It's a winter wonderland today. This Texas boy wants to enjoy it." He squeezed my fingers, making the Mentos bubbles work their way into every vein in my body.

I huddled deeper into my coat as he pulled me toward the Ag building. With snow covering everything, campus did appear magical. Powder outlined the artistic shape of trees. A foggy mist hung in the air. Even the way our breath frosted in front of our faces dazzled me.

"Are you busy after work?" he asked.

I extracted my gloved hand from his. Who cared if the snow made campus stunning? Parker had a girlfriend, so this wasn't kosher. We shouldn't be alone together. What if Lily happened to see him with me? I mean, it'd serve her right since she'd cheated on him, but I didn't want to be the *other* woman.

"I have to study for a calc test."

He stroked my cheek with his free hand.

I gulped. "W-what are you doing?"

His thumb moved along my jaw, and though I knew it was wrong, I couldn't move away. Alone with Parker in a frozen wonderland, he became a concertmaster, leading a full-scale symphony orchestra inside of me with just the touch of his hand.

"I don't know," he whispered. "I've never felt this way before." His thumb continued to explore the contours of my face, making me feel as beautiful as the inner ensemble he created.

But he was taken. Out of reach.

I turned my head. "I-I have to go back."

"Can I see you tomorrow?" He caught my hand again.

I swallowed to moisten my parched throat. "I-I work."

"Then I'll walk with you on your break again." He squeezed my fingers, sending the bubbles into a spiraling tingle-fest as my beating heart and trumpeting emotions joined his stirring symphony.

Parker kept stroking my hand on the way back to the shop. I loved it, but knew this wasn't real. He loved his Barbie doll. Maybe they'd had a fight and had split up momentarily. Or he pitied me. Either option sucked. I didn't want pity, and I certainly didn't want to be his rebound until he crawled back to Lily. Because he would.

But heaven help me, I couldn't pull my hand away from him.

28

PARKER

$\mathcal{M}$Y KNEE BOUNCED as I waited in the library lobby for Meridee to arrive. Yesterday's walk during her break had been fun. I'd teased her, and she'd tried hard not to smile. But I'd won a few laughs from her. With the big game today though, I'd asked if we could meet earlier to walk since I had to be at the stadium by two.

I spotted her on the outside steps and hurried over to open the glass doors for her. "Hey, Mare."

"Hey."

I longed to reach out and touch her adorable freckles. Instead, I put my arm out and asked, "Elbow or hand?"

She rolled her eyes. "Neither."

She'd said that yesterday, too, and had kept hands in her pockets or arms folded the whole walk. I asked mostly because I enjoyed seeing her blush.

We walked along the cleared sidewalk, and Meridee dug her gloved hands deeper into her coat pockets.

"How was class?"

"It was—" She yelped as her boot hit a patch of black ice. Her arms flailed and she started to go down.

I grabbed her by the waist to steady her, but my Vans could gain no traction on the treacherous path. I yanked her against me and somehow managed to keep us both from landing on our backsides. But now, our bodies were mashed together like sardines in a can, except without the

128

stink. My heart beat double time as our noses touched. Though the temperature sat below freezing, sweat formed along my spine from all the fires Mare ignited inside me. I inhaled her sweet scent as our gazes locked.

How had I not noticed her last year when I'd visited Ferdinand's? Talk about being blind.

But I was fully aware of her now.

"Sorry." She sounded as breathless as I felt. "I-I slipped."

"Me, too."

She squirmed in my arms.

"Maybe you should take my arm so you don't slip again. You almost took me out."

She made a face. "Or we could return to the library."

"Where's the fun in that? Come on." I put out my arm.

"Okay." She threaded her arm through mine.

I inwardly cheered as I guided her across the street. "What do you want to do when you graduate? Work in a gym?" Her major was exercise science.

"Nutrition and exercise physiology is a pre-med degree. I'm not out to give Jillian Michaels competition. I hope to get accepted into Duke for their physician's assistant program. It's one of the top in the nation."

"Ah." How had I not known that? I'd just latched onto the word *exercise* and had made assumptions. "Working at the hospital makes sense now."

"I need to transition to full-time there eventually, but I haven't been able to make the break from Ferdinand's. That place saved me when I moved here after my divorce. Made me feel capable again."

I squeezed her arm, sensing her unease.

She stiffened. "What about you? I heard the announcer discuss your NFL prospects during last week's game. Will you keep playing football?"

I stopped. "You watched my last game?"

Her cheeks turned a cute reddish hue. "Bryce had it on his phone at work. I couldn't help but see a few plays."

"And you didn't write him up?"

She elbowed me. "You sound like Mr. Owens. Everyone wanted updates, so I figured it was good customer service to keep tabs on the game."

I tried not to gloat. Mare would become a fan yet.

"Answer my question," she said.

I grimaced. "Everybody wants me to enter the draft."

"What do you want?"

"Truthfully, the NFL would be cool, but I've dealt with shoulder pain the last two seasons. The trainer keeps me functioning, but I worry I wouldn't last long in the pros before I injured it worse, maybe permanently."

"Then don't do it."

I smiled. "Thank you. You're the first person, besides my mom, who hasn't made me feel like a fool for not wanting to go pro."

"What do you want to do instead?"

"Work in avionics."

"Building airplanes?"

"Not quite. Avionics are the electronic systems used in airplanes or satellites. I'd like to work for a company like Boeing. Do communications, navigation, tactical systems, stuff like that."

"Cool."

We reached a flight of stairs, and I acted on impulse and swept her into my arms. She was just so dang cute and irresistible.

"What are you doing?" she cried. "Put me down."

"No way, my lady. These stairs are too dangerous. But never fear, your handsome knight will carry you up so you don't fall and break your noggin'."

The goofy English accent made her laugh as I jogged to the top. Mare fit perfectly in my arms, like she'd been made specifically for them.

I set her on her feet. "That was great exercise. Maybe I should carry you up these stairs every day until next week's game to get in shape."

"You're still playing? Isn't the season over?"

Only Mare would be so clueless. "Tonight's game and next week's will be the last for season play." I gazed into her mesmerizing brown eyes, noticing flecks of gold. "Then we should know which bowl we'll play in at the end of December or early January. Pray we get the Holiday Bowl. San Diego's warm." I leaned closer, but she tensed up. Again. She seemed to do that a lot.

I eased back, not wanting to spook her. A gust of wind whipped through my coat. "Brrr. It's chilly."

Her eyes crinkled up at the corners. "You're just noticing that?"

I winked. "I don't notice much else when I'm with you." I propped my elbow out, and she linked arms without an argument. Progress. "Thanks for walking with me."

She caught the side of her lip in her teeth.

I gulped, wishing to take over that job for her.

"It was fun." She tugged at her wool hat when we returned to the library. "I better go. See you later."

"Hey," I called. When she turned, I said, "Can I stop by the hospital sometime this week? I have footballs for each of the kids."

She gave me a full-on smile. Wow. Maybe I'd go to the hospital every day, if that was her reaction.

"They'd love that."

I took out my phone and texted her.

She looked down and shook her head at my message. "I meant to ask you earlier how you got my number. Did Riley give it to you?"

"I'm sure you programmed it in there when I wasn't looking," I teased.

She giggled.

"Text me when your next hospital shift is. I'll play delivery boy."

"Thanks, Parker."

"Thank you."

I watched until she disappeared, then threw my fist into the air. *Yes!*

29

MERIDEE

I YAWNED AND stretched my arms, thinking of Parker's earlier game. I'd caved and let Sean keep the game playing on his phone during our shift. During the last minute of the fourth quarter, Parker had stolen the ball from the other team—I think Sean had called it an interception, and he'd screamed so loud that my ears still rang. I'd watched with bated breath as Parker had run almost the entire length of the field to score a touchdown. He'd looked amazing, and I hadn't been able to banish the image of his huge grin from my mind, even after I'd climbed into bed.

I jumped when my phone beeped with a text from the same guy I'd been thinking about.

How's studying?

I rubbed my head. Why the sudden interest in me—the hand-holding during our walks and the carrying me up the stairs yesterday? I treasured Parker's friendship. I did. He made me laugh and feel comfortable, which hadn't happened with any other guy besides my brother. Except Parker was not my brother, and I had the opposite of sisterly feelings for him.

I hate calculus. :(

*Need help? I'm in
2nd semester.*

I pursed my lips. Popular, handsome, *and* smart. Why couldn't he have a fatal flaw?

> *No hope at this point.*
> *Test at 8 am. Can you*
> *give me a new brain?*

Ul do fine.

I leaned over my desk, wondering why he wanted to hang out when he could be with his Barbie getting hot, steamy lip action.

Have I told u how crazy
I am 4u?

Don't read anything into his words, I told myself. He only considered me a friend. The hand-holding and playful pecks didn't mean anything to him. Parker was affectionate. I'd observed him with his girlfriend and knew what he acted like when he was serious. That's not how he treated me.

> *Have I told you what*
> *an idiot you are?*

Maybe sarcasm would put an end to his foolishness.

But m I ur idiot?

What did he mean by that?

> *Go to bed. Lily*
> *wouldn't like you*
> *texting other girls.*

Lily's history.
Ur my present.

> *I need to study. And it's*
> *YOU'RE, not UR.*

Texting tip 1:
shortn wut u can.

I scratched my head. What did he mean by Lily being history? Had they broken up? I didn't see that lasting long. He'd admitted how easily she distracted him. She'd figure out a way to get her man back.

My phone kept dinging with new texts, but I didn't respond. It took two to play his game, and I'd be safer sitting the bench.

10:52
I thank God every day I
went after that throw in
the cafeteria and ran u over.

10:53
Do u want 2 meet 4 lunch 2moro?

10:54
I h8 when u ignore me.

11:01
RU done studying?

11:03
I could help. I love calc.

11:05
Mare, don't ignore me. Pleez!

11:06
I really m crazy 4U. No joke.

11:08
Id rather throw a football than
these texts. Plus Ur not
throwing NE returns.

11:09
Have u evr broken NE bones?

11:09
Iv broken 6.

11:10
Bet Uv nevr broken NE.
MI right?

I closed my book and gave in to the determined man. Studying wasn't happening tonight.

> *I broke my toe in*
> *3rd grade PE.*

Ah, she returns to the
world of texting.
Toes don't count.

> *Ha, ha. Go to bed.*

Can't. I'm studying.

> *What are you studying that*
> *you have time to text*
> *me every minute?*

R relationship.

> *LOL. We don't have*
> *a relationship.*

Im hoping 2 start 1.

> *You're delusional. Go*
> *let Barbie distract you.*

No way in HE-- M I
getting back with that
B--. Biggest mistake evr.

*Says all the guys before
they get back with her.*

*Serious, Mare. I like u.
Not just like, but
LIKE-LIKE.*

*You need to stop texting
things you'll regret
in the morning.*

*Do u like me a little?
U let me hold ur hand.*

*Who doesn't like you?
The whole campus likes you.*

Look outside.

What was he up to now? I threw open the door and stepped onto my balcony. Flashing lights drew my attention to the parking lot as my phone rang and Parker's face popped up on the screen.

"What are you doing?" I answered.

"My truck's waving at you. Wave back."

I shook my head at the blinking lights and returned to my room.

He chuckled on the other end. "Ah, Mare, why won't you have any fun with me?"

"Go home." I didn't want to be his rebound girl. My heart wouldn't survive.

"I forgot to give you something earlier. Come out and get it."

"I'm in my pajamas."

"The sexy sheep ones?"

"No, dork. It's freezing cold."

"Bundle up and hurry down. My heater doesn't work too well in this old truck."

Knowing the stubborn man wouldn't give up, I threw on a robe and grabbed snow boots. "Fine. I'm coming." I'd go get whatever he had and send him on his way. Then I'd go to bed and forget about tonight's weirdness. He must be beyond bored.

I marched into the frosty night as Parker kept flashing his lights. He stepped out of his old truck and gave me one of his Mr. Universe smiles, making me all warm inside.

Those smiles. They always got to me.

"What did you forget to give me?"

Parker erased the distance between us in two giant steps, pulling me into his arms. "This." Before I could blink or think, he leaned in and covered my mouth with his.

I stiffened as his soft lips plied mine. But as his hands rubbed me through my robe, I slowly relaxed. My mind hiccuped for joy.

Parker was kissing me. Really kissing me!

His kiss didn't plunder and conquer as I expected. He was gentle. Tender, even. I'd never dreamed a kiss could feel so incredible. So addicting. His hands didn't ravage. They caressed and soothed, making every inch of my skin tingle. Though short, his kiss left me trembling and dazed when he pulled away.

"I wanted to give you that earlier. Shoot." He licked his lips. "I've wanted to kiss you since the weekend we spent with my mom."

"But...you have a girlfriend." I said it more for my benefit than his. His kiss had been amazing, tempting me to pull him back for more.

"Not for a month. I'm my own man now, doing what I want to do for freaking once." He winked and climbed back into his truck. "Sweet dreams, Mare."

My face burned with happiness, not the smarting sting from one of Brody's slaps. I waved as Parker honked and pulled away and I floated back to my apartment, thankful my roommates were still out. I didn't want to explain my flushed face and giddy smile. I didn't quite understand them myself.

But I did know I'd have very sweet dreams tonight.

30

PARKER

ULLING MY HOODIE over my head, I waited around the corner from Meridee's calculus class. I had the next hour free and wanted to spend it with her before I had to go to physics. Students filed out of classrooms at ten to the hour. I lowered my head and hid behind a book to keep from being recognized. The last season game this coming weekend had everyone on campus stoked. Everyone except Meridee.

I smiled as I recalled last night's kiss. It'd been a whole different experience than kissing Lily. Better. I'd appreciated Mare's innocence and wonder. Who knew that'd be so much more of a turn-on than Lily's vast experience?

When I spotted Meridee's unique golden-brown hair in the crowd, I stashed my book in my bag and caught up to her.

"Howdy, darling," I said in her ear.

She flinched as I grabbed her hand. Another student recognized me and shouted my name. I nodded to acknowledge him but lowered my head and detoured down an empty corridor lined with offices. When we were alone, I stopped and faced her.

"How did you do on your test?"

She bit her lip. The vulnerable gesture reminded me how delicious she'd tasted last night.

"It was difficult, but I feel good. How did you find me?"

I hugged her, making her stiffen again. "I played the part of spy and followed you from your apartment."

Her eyes crinkled. "Stalker."

"You up for lunch?"

She nodded. "I'm starving."

I clasped hands, pulled my hoodie up over my head again, and we walked out the doors together. "How about orange chicken?"

She giggled.

We made our way through the crowded CUB, and I ordered orange chicken for both of us and carried it to an out-of-the-way corner table.

Mare gaped at me as I dug into my double order. "How can you eat all that?"

"How can I not? I burn at least three thousand calories at practice and am always half-starved."

She took a bite of chicken and rice. "Crazy."

I raised my Coke. "To orange chicken."

She clinked her styrofoam cup of lemonade against my aluminum can. "May it always be in my mouth, not my hair and clothes."

I snickered. "But it looked so good on you."

The next hour passed like Jeff Gordon down the Daytona Speedway. We ate, laughed, and talked about everything and nothing. I reached across the table and took her hand.

"Do you have any more classes?" she asked.

"In ten minutes. I wish I could skip, but this physics test counts for twenty percent of my grade."

She yanked her hand away. "Ten minutes! Why did you let me talk to you for so long? You need to go."

I scooted my chair closer, trapping her against the wall. "First things first." Physics could wait. I caressed her adorable freckled cheek.

Meridee's thick lashes fluttered. "P-Parker, I don't want to be responsible for you missing your test."

I leaned over for the kill, but she pushed me away. "Not here."

My gaze dropped to her lips. "After my test?"

She licked her tasty lips. "Only if you get an A. And only in private."

I winked. "I promise to get an A plus-plus."

I pecked her cheek before heading to class.

The next two hours dragged by as I tried to recall formulas and equations and work through the five intense problems my professor had created. When I finished, I headed to the parking lot with a spring in my step as I considered Meridee's sweet lips and how much pressure I could apply to them for maximum pleasure and relationship acceleration.

Physics principles should be applied to be understood.
I couldn't wait to put them into practice.

31

MERIDEE

*W*INDY, CURVY ROADS always made me nervous. And I'd been on edge before I'd gotten in the truck with Parker. I couldn't believe this was really happening. Parker had picked me up after class, insisting we drive up into the hills outside of town. For privacy. I guess I had only myself to blame for that one.

I squirmed, trying once more to figure out why he liked me. Or did he? Had I'd blown last night's kiss into something it wasn't? It'd been my dream come true, but maybe it hadn't meant anything to him. Maybe he kissed every girl he hung out with.

Parker patted the middle spot. "You're thinking too much. Scoot over so we're warmer."

My heart pounded like a drummer in a hard rock band as I obeyed. Parker threw an arm over my shoulders. I'd considered the gesture sweet when he'd done it to his mom, but now I found it maddeningly distracting.

But I shouldn't give too much weight to his actions. This was Parker Harrington. Football star. Ladies' man. Biggest flirt on campus. I needed to guard my heart. But as his fingers stroked my arm—back and forth, back and forth—I snuggled closer.

He pulled off onto a dirt road and parked under snow-laden pines. I folded my arms to contain my excitement. I'd always longed to come up to Kamiak Butte, but my brother had been too busy with classes and labs to ever bring me, and I'd never had a boyfriend to drive me up to this scenic spot. I focused on the distant hills, wondering if Parker would try to kiss me again. I both hoped he would and wouldn't.

He kept his truck running but tilted his head to rest again mine. A gasping wheeze escaped as my muscles tensed.

He eased back to look in my eyes. "What's the happiest moment of your life?"

I gave him a silly answer. "When I got my braces off in the middle of my senior year."

"Really?"

I grinned, showing off my straight teeth. "I hated being called Brace Face."

"Kids didn't call you that, did they?"

I shrugged. "I wasn't Miss Popular, like you. I'm still not." I chewed my lip. Would that bother him? "What about you? What's your happiest moment?"

"Our kiss last night. No contest."

"Don't be a dork."

"I'm not. It made me extremely happy." He raised both brows. "But I'm curious to see if I can top it."

A shaky breath escaped me. "Y-you are?"

He took off his gloves and tugged mine off as well so he could play with my bare fingers. I shivered, but not from the frigid temperature. This was really happening. Parker was going to kiss me again. His hands were warm, yet I automatically tensed when he moved his fingers to my face.

I closed my eyes, held my breath, and waited for contact.

"Mare?" His minty breath caressed my lips.

I opened my eyes to find him watching me. "Y-yes?"

"What did Brody do to you?"

At the mention of my ex, I pulled out of his arms, chest squeezing painfully.

"Oh, Mare." He pulled me back into his embrace, but comfort fueled his intent now, not passion.

The snowy hills blurred into gray, blue, and white brush strokes as tears escaped. Parker caressed my hair as I buried deeper into his chest and shuddered. I don't know how long I silently cried as he held me, but when the tidal wave of emotions passed, I felt better.

"Sorry." I swiped at my eyes.

"Don't be. My shoulder's here for you whenever you need a good cry."

I cursed my volatile emotions. So much for romance. I'd ruined the mood completely.

He wrapped an arm around me. "Want to talk about it?"

I shook my head. That was the last thing I wanted to do.

"May I ask one question?"

I gulped. "You can ask." I might not answer.

"Is he the reason you flinch and tense up whenever I get close?"

I looked out the window, humiliated that he'd noticed. I tried not to freak out when he touched me. Really, I did. I thought I'd succeeded. But obviously not enough.

Parker tipped my chin. "Of course, once I started kissing you last night, you melted like a marshmallow over a campfire."

I smiled at his teasing. "Your kiss was nicer than Brody's."

"Nicer? That's all I rate? We need to change that."

"How do you"—I swallowed—"intend to do that?" My cheeks burned. Flirting didn't come natural to me.

He leaned closer, and my body reacted like a box of fireworks in a nuclear reactor. My pulse skyrocketed as I blinked to keep from revealing the pleasurable chaos happening inside me.

"I'm open to suggestions." His lips hovered above mine, but he didn't take. He waited, making desire wash over me like warm water.

I closed my eyes. "You could"—I gulped—"kiss me again."

"Brilliant idea. I did ace my physics test."

His lips rested on mine, gently increasing the pressure as a virtuoso might coax music from a dusty violin that'd sat in an attic for too long. I inhaled his musky scent and shivered. This is what most people must feel when they kissed. Brody had been a poor imitation.

Parker's tongue slid along the seam of my lips, and I moaned and opened to him. My shoulders relaxed as yearning flared to life and conquered the residual fear I'd clung to for so long. Parker's kiss took various twists and delicious turns, but with such delicate grace and gentle wonder that I didn't feel used.

I felt cherished.

Adored.

Treasured.

His tender ministrations bolstered my confidence. I reached up to take his face in my hands, exploring his chiseled jaw and rubbing my finger against his moist lips. Touching a man's face and watching his breathing hitch and speed up at my touch thrilled me. Never had I initiated contact with Brody, fearing him like a loaded gun. But as I ran my fingers along

Parker's neck, face, and up through his hair, I reveled in the power I seemed to hold over him. He pulled me closer in a desperate need to erase the distance between us, and we took turns savoring each other.

When Parker pulled away, I couldn't stop grinning. He caressed my cheek. I cradled his hand against my skin. For years, I'd avoided men, fearing their touch. But today, Parker had taught me that a man's touch could heal as well as hurt.

"I've never felt this way before," he said.

"Even with Lily?" I couldn't contain my curiosity...or envy.

He shook his head. "We had chemistry, but not much else." He ran his fingers through my hair again. "This is beautiful."

I wrinkled my nose. Lily hadn't struck me as nice, but she was perfect-looking. Most guys would be willing to forgive a world of faults because of that.

"Did you really break up with her?"

He scowled. "I wouldn't be kissing you if I hadn't. My mama taught me better than that."

"Sorry." I licked my still-tingling lips. "I had to know."

"There's no one else but you." He touched my cheek. "I really like you, Mare. I have for a while. You worked your way into my heart when you were dating Riley, and I haven't been able to stop thinking about you. You're amazing."

Too bad I couldn't bottle up his words and preserve them forever.

He wrapped an arm around my shoulder and pulled me in so I could rest my head against him again. "I'm glad you're my girlfriend now, not his."

I tilted my head. "Am I your girlfriend?" That seemed too impossible to believe.

He nuzzled my ear. "I guess I assumed you were after that mind-blowing kiss." He winked as I blushed. "We should probably make it official so you don't wonder anymore." He took my hands in his. "Meridee, any guy would love you for your cooking, but I've fallen for the girl behind the apron. I love how easy you are to talk to, how much you love those kids at the hospital, and how you treat me like a normal guy, not some freaking celebrity."

I tried to stifle a full-on smile.

"Will you be my girl?" He raised both brows.

"Are you serious?"

"Did my kiss not convey that?" He gave me a goofy grin.

Happiness erupted inside me, and I laughed and wrapped my arms around him. "Then yes! I'll be your girl. If you're sure."

"I'm one hundred percent certain." Parker captured my lips once more, giving me a kiss that chased away all remaining doubts.

This time, I didn't tense up or fear what he might do. I closed my eyes and enjoyed every thrilling touch of his lips against mine and the way his hands caressed my sensitive body. Every inch of me tingled with pleasure as I reciprocated with my whole heart.

This kiss was a new beginning, not an exploratory testing of the waters. A kiss to spark my inner bowstrings and his radiant notes into a full-scale symphony of the heart.

I lost track of time, of the cold, of the lovely surroundings. Parker could've kissed me all day and it wouldn't have been long enough. Never had I felt so strongly for a man before, and I couldn't get enough of him now that these feelings had been freed inside me.

Parker pulled away breathless, but kept his forehead glued to mine. "Do you think I'm serious now?" He gave me a mischievous grin.

I rubbed my nose against his. "Uh-huh."

"Good, because I don't want to stop kissing my girlfriend."

I giggled as he kissed me again.

We savored each other even more, and when he pulled away, I snuggled against him and sighed as his fingers played with mine. We cuddled for a long time, soaking in the peaceful surroundings and stealing more kisses. I couldn't get over how comfortable I felt with him. We didn't even need to talk.

His phone rang.

"Sorry." He straightened. "It's my roommate. Let me take this."

I pulled my gloves on and listened to his one-sided conversation as I compared Parker to my ex. I'd believed Brody cared for me in the beginning, but it'd never been like this. Not even close. In my innocence, I'd believed Brody's aggressive mouth and groping hands were a normal part of a guy-girl relationship. Something I must endure. I'd assumed the problem rested with me and had focused on how lucky I was to have such a handsome guy's attention. But Parker didn't take as Brody had. He gave, and I'd become a very greedy girlfriend in the short time since he'd made things official between us.

Parker hung up. "My roommate has a friend who's willing to buy my contract next semester."

"That's great. Now you can move in with Riley."

"Yeah. He wants to meet tonight after ten, so I won't be able to meet you after work, but I'll pick you up first thing in the morning and we'll do breakfast. Sound good?"

I nodded. Morning couldn't come soon enough. "I'll keep my fingers crossed for you."

He leaned over to kiss me, and we became absorbed in each other again. When we came up for air, I noted the time on the dashboard.

"Shoot! I have to be at Ferdinand's in thirty minutes."

Parker nuzzled my cheek. "Guess I'd better drive you home."

I snuggled against him on the way back to town, feeling safe with his arm around me.

He was nothing like Brody. Ours had been a whirlwind courtship, where I hadn't had time to consider or really get to know him before we'd stood before a Vegas preacher, repeating vows Brody never had intended to keep.

Parker was different. He made me feel beautiful and wanted, not useless and betrayed.

In front of my apartment building, he leaned over to kiss the top of my head. "I wish I could hang out at Ferdinand's with you."

"I wouldn't get anything done if you did. All I'd think about is kissing you."

He tucked his finger under my chin. "So you like kissing me?"

I bit my lips. "You know I do."

"I like kissing you, too. A lot." His brow furrowed as he ran a finger over my cheek. "I promise I'll never hurt you."

I threaded my fingers through his. "I know."

His lips joined mine, sealing his words with action. When I shivered, he hugged me.

"This old truck isn't built for these types of winters. It wants the heat and dirt of the Texas desert." He rubbed my arms. "Let's get you inside."

He walked me to my door, where we kissed again. I'd probably be late, but who cared? I really enjoyed kissing my new boyfriend.

"See you first thing in the morning." He brushed his lips against my cheek, making me tremble. "I'll miss you."

I would miss him, too. More than he would ever know.

All I wanted was for tomorrow to get here so I could be with Parker again and receive more spine-tingling, soul-enhancing, symphony-inspiring kisses.

When the slowest shift of my life ended, I applied a light shade of pink to my lips in the break room and smacked them together. I'd asked Bryce to close up with Sean so I could leave a few minutes early, and I'd shoved a ten-dollar bill into the till to pay for a tub of non-expired Huckleberry Ripple.

Time to put my daring plan into action.

I grabbed my purse and walked out to Sean's whistle.

"Where are you going all dolled up?" He waggled his brows. "Are you meeting a certain football player by chance?"

"None of your business." I laughed on my way out the door.

"Tell Sticky Fingers Hi from me," he yelled. "And that I'll be cheering for him the weekend."

"You and every other person on campus." It still shocked me how nutso everyone on campus was for this upcoming game.

I chewed my lips like a beaver on the drive to Parker's. Never did I do unexpected, random things like show up at a guy's apartment uninvited. I was a rule-follower, a planner. But after spending the afternoon with Parker, I felt like a new woman. Free. Happy. Daring. Stepping out of my comfort zone would prove I was invested in this relationship. And surely, the ice cream would thrill him, even if he was too tired to hang out.

The weather had warmed, but plenty of snow still lined the sides of the road. My teeth ripped skin off my lip, making me wince. If I wanted any color left for Parker to kiss off, I needed to stop biting them.

I pulled into a parking space and did some breathing patterns to calm myself. I shouldn't be nervous. This was Parker. He liked me. After what we'd shared this afternoon, how could I doubt that?

I leaned up to check my face in the rear-view mirror. A dab of lip gloss gave some shine to my lips. I gave myself the Nike pep talk—*Just do it*—and grabbed the tub of ice cream.

Movement on an upper level caught my eye as I opened my door. Parker emerged from what must be his apartment.

I sank back into my seat, one foot on the asphalt, admiring my handsome boyfriend in the glow of the porch light. He really was a Nordic god. He leaned against the railing, facing his open door as he talked to someone inside.

Should I wait, or call out to him? I hadn't bargained on other people being with him.

A stunning blonde walked out and wrapped her arms around him, and my heart turned to stone and crumbled to pieces. Tears gathered in mass, stinging my eyes and back of my throat as she reached up to kiss him.

I closed my eyes, pain bludgeoning me as surely as if Brody had shoved my head against a wall.

Parker had lied.

There was no guy there trying to buy his contract. He was with Lily, and they didn't appear broke-up at all.

Dreams disintegrated into dewy tears. I bowed my head as a gut-wrenching groan tightened my ab muscles. Like Brody, Parker had taken what he wanted and tossed me aside. I was only a conquest, or a rebound, by the looks of it.

Why had I believed I could be anything more?

I looked up to find the landing empty. Lily was gone. Parker, too. Maybe they'd walked back inside to enjoy a passionate night of spine-tingling kisses. Parker excelled at those. I wished I didn't have firsthand knowledge of that now. It'd been much easier to keep my feelings in check when he'd only been an imaginary boyfriend. Not the cheater that had been exposed tonight.

PARKER

$\mathcal{T}$HE LECTURE CONCLUDED, and I stuffed my notes into my backpack and texted Mare to see if she was done with class. She'd texted earlier to bail on breakfast since she hadn't felt well.

Not the best start to my day.

She replied in the negative seconds later.

No.

Call when UR.

I sprinkled on a few heart emojis before pocketing my phone and exiting the auditorium.

The hallway was filled with girls and guys alike, who acted as though I was special just because I could catch a pigskin. I'd be glad when the season ended. I wanted my life back.

At Riley's apartment, I microwaved a frozen lasagna and kept checking my phone for Mare's reply. Finally, I could take it no more and texted her again.

U done?

Not til 2.

I frowned. Since when did she have classes until two? That wouldn't give me any time to hang out with her before practice. And I really wanted to see how she was faring, being sick and all.

What about work?

I called in sick.

Good. I'll come over after practice.

Stay clear. You don't want to catch this bug.

Worth it 2B with U. Will U watch my game Saturday?

You have plenty of fans watching already.

Only 1 I care about. Her name rhymes w/care bear. BTW have I told u how much I <3 u?

Tell someone who cares.

I winced. Texting didn't always convey emotions, but her reply had come off quite harsh. Not Meridee-like at all. Her cold must've thrown off her cheery mojo. I pushed my plate aside, bummed that I couldn't see her before practice so I could kiss her for good luck.

"Bad news?" Riley asked as he entered the kitchen.

I rolled my shoulder. "Mare's sick."

"That sucks."

"Yeah. I think I'll stop by and see her after practice, so I'll be back late." I didn't care what she said, I'd take care of my girl. Bring her dinner. Give her a back rub if she still felt icky. Kiss her thoroughly if she felt better.

Riley grabbed his duffel bag. "Ready to head?"

I rolled my other shoulder. "Sure. Let me grab my gear." It'd be a long, grueling afternoon, prepping for the big game.

The next few hours crept by like a snail over a tack board. I stretched with the trainer and worked with Coach and the rest of the offensive team on a new play we planned to throw into the game to keep Nevada from shutting me down.

After practice ended, I picked up comfort food on my way to Mare's apartment. Maybe she'd be wearing those gray flannel pajamas tonight. It'd be fun to cuddle her in those. Never had I met a girl I was so comfortable around. Mom must've prayed her on me and sent me crashing into her that day in the CUB.

Mare's giddy roommate opened the door and gave me a weird look.

"Hey. Is Meridee here?" The stacked containers leaned precariously in my arms.

"She's not."

"Really? Do you know where she went?" Maybe she was feeling better.

She frowned, and I wondered why she wasn't bouncing and giggling as usual. "Did you guys fight?"

"No." Why would she ask that?

She motioned me inside. I stepped into the living room and noticed that all of the poppy paintings were gone. The walls were stark and bare, like move-out day. There were still three weeks left in the semester, but maybe Mare and her roommates had gotten an early start on clean-check.

The brunette picked up a letter on the table and handed it to me. I set it on top of my Styrofoam containers.

"I don't know what happened, but Meridee moved out and told me to give you this if you came by."

"She moved out?" I stared at the envelope that had my name written in block letters. She hadn't ever mentioned that she had to move out today.

"This morning. Last night I found her sobbing in her room and asked what was wrong, but she wouldn't say. I assumed you guys fought. I know she liked you, even if she pretended she didn't."

I scratched my head. "No. I dropped her off happy." At least, I'd assumed she'd been happy. I surely had been. "Could she have received bad news from home?"

The roommate shrugged. "I have no idea, but she was up before six loading her car with her belongings. She gave me this letter and left."

My stomach churned. Mare's earlier texts had mentioned nothing about moving out. What had happened?

151

"Okay. Thanks." I made my way back to the parking lot.

In the privacy of my truck, I ripped open the letter and swore as I read Mare's slanted script. Dropping the paper, I pulled out my phone and tried to call her. When she didn't answer, I sent a text.

Got ur letter. It's not what
U think. Please call me.

I waited several minutes, but she didn't respond.

I jogged back to her apartment and pounded on the door.

"Do you know where she went?" I asked, when the same roommate answered.

"Sorry. I'm just as weirded out by this as you are. She didn't say a word to any of us."

I returned to my truck and laid my head against the steering wheel. Where could she have gone? I had to find Mare and fix this.

At Ferdinand's, I pounded on the locked doors until Sean let me into the empty shop. He told me Mare had quit that morning, not even giving two weeks' notice.

My heart sank, drowning. Only Mare could save me. She'd loved her job at Ferdinand's. I couldn't believe she'd just up and quit. I had to find her ASAP!

I staggered into Riley's apartment, still clutching Mare's letter.

He glanced up from the couch, where he was watching game highlights on ESPN. "What's the matter with you, man?"

I sank into the cushions and handed him the letter. As he read, I skimmed the words over his shoulder again.

Parker,
You're the same betraying, lying, SOB as Brody. Thankfully, I found
out the truth about you before it was too late. Thank Barbie for me for
that. I don't want to see you again. I've moved and blocked your
number, so don't waste time trying to find me to give me a sweet-
tongued lie I'm too smart to believe. It's over...not that you have much
to get over, since you seemed plenty distracted with Barbie tonight. But
I'm out of this twisted game.
Meridee

Riley winced. "Ouch."

"She must've driven over to my apartment last night and saw me with Lily."

Riley frowned. "Dude, I thought you broke up with her."

"I did."

"Then why did Meridee see you with her?"

My nostrils flared. "My roommate called and said he had a buyer for my contract. But he lied. It was a setup. Lily was waiting for me in my room instead."

Riley scowled.

I put my hands in the air. "I didn't do anything. I ran out onto the balcony and yelled for her to put her clothes on and leave. She wasn't happy, but when I refused to come in, she finally left. But she hugged me. Started crying and apologizing for cheating on me. Said she'd made a huge mistake. I didn't want to smack her when she was down, so I hugged her back. And she kissed me quick. That's all. I didn't kiss her back, but Mare must've driven over and seen us together. But I swear on the Bible, all I did was try to comfort her."

"Comfort?"

I grimaced. "I patted her back, told her I forgave her, walked her to her car. When she tried to kiss me again, I made it clear I wasn't ever getting back together with her. I told her I loved someone else." I gulped. "You believe me, don't you?"

Riley nodded. "Yeah, but that doesn't help you get Meridee back if you have no way to tell her the truth."

I cracked my knuckles. "I have to find her, Ry."

"Pull yourself together, man. What's her number? I deleted it when she broke up with me."

I met his gaze. "You'll call her for me?"

"Yeah. I'll explain and try to convince her to talk to you."

I threw my head against the back of the couch. "Thanks, man."

"Don't thank me yet."

I gave him her number and waited.

"Uh, hi, Meridee," Riley said when she answered. "Uh, no? Well, yeah. He's sitting right here, actually. No, no!" he cried. "Listen, please." He frowned and looked up at me. "She hung up on me."

I snatched the phone from him and hit redial. It rang and rang and rang. When her sweet voice came on saying to leave a message at the beep, I did just that.

"Mare, about what you saw. It's not what you think. I never invited Lily over. She set me up. I swear. I showed up and found her in my bedroom. I ran outside and told her to leave. I know it looked bad, but nothing happened. She wanted to get back together, but I told her no way that would happen, because I'm in love with someone else. You." I released a long breath. "I'm not playing games, Mare. I swear. I'm more serious than I've ever been in my life. I adore you. Please call me back. Please."

I hit *End* and sank into the couch. "Do you think she'll call?"

Riley shrugged. "Better question is: Will she listen to the message?"

TOUCHDOWN

33

MERIDEE

*M*Y REFUGE HAD become a lone bench in the corner of the second floor of Cleveland Hall. Here I could work on homework or eat a snack among education students without worrying that Parker might find me. After discovering the cheater with Barbie four days ago, I'd packed up my apartment and had moved into my aunt's basement in Colfax. The arrangement wasn't ideal since it added twenty-five minutes to my commute each way and a bratty eleven-year-old cousin to deal with, but I could not—dared not—see Parker Harrington again. He'd crushed every resurrected crumb of trust I had in men. In humanity.

The stupid man had turned my life completely upside down. Not only did I have to live off campus now—in another city, no less—but I had to watch my step on campus to keep from running into him. He seemed to be everywhere. I'd spied him craning his neck as he searched the crowds in the science building, where most of my classes were. I'd almost bumped into him on my way to my practicum lecture. I'd had to find new employment, since he could've found me too easily at Ferdinand's. He'd proven how stubborn he could be when he wanted to see me. Though I didn't know why he bothered. I was just a joke to him.

Miriam had agreed to give me twenty hours at the hospital if I worked graveyard shift. So I was exhausted on top of all the other changes. The shift in jobs had needed to happen, but I still hated Parker for pushing my timeline forward.

I squirmed to find a more comfortable position on the unyielding bench and opened my physiology and anatomy book. But my eyelids kept closing. My new schedule would take some getting used to.

I must've dozed, because when I blinked awake, I had the hair-raising sensation of being watched. Sitting up, I flinched when I discovered a muscular guy on the floor, leaning against my bench.

I yelped, sending my textbook flying.

"Hey, Meridee." Riley returned my book to me.

"Oh, hey. Sorry." I took a deep breath to slow my heart rate. "You startled me. H-how are you?" *And why are you here?*

"I'm fine." He put his arms behind his head. "But I know someone who's not."

I narrowed my eyes.

"Parker's miserable," he said. "I've never seen him so depressed. He drags about each day as though he carries the weight of the world on his shoulders. He doesn't smile. Hardly eats. He's sucking it up at practice. I'm really worried for this game tomorrow. Every free second he has, he's searching for you, hoping to plead his case."

I hugged my chest. "I don't want to hear any more of his lies. How did you find me?"

"Just lucky. I came here to surprise my girl and walk her to lunch, but spotted you instead, and wa-lah!" He gave me a crooked grin. "Here we are."

"Now I have to find a new place to study." Dang it!

"Don't. I'm not lying about Parker being miserable since you left him."

"You say that as if I'm the bad guy. I didn't cheat on him. I believed he cared about me and..." I pinched my eyelids.

He touched my shoulder. "He does care about you. I know you saw him with Lily, but he actually ousted her from his apartment. She came over uninvited. When she left, she hugged him."

"He seemed only too glad to hug her back. And kiss her."

"She apologized for cheating and turned on the tears. He was just being nice. Nothing romantic. Honestly, Lily doesn't have a chance now that he's fallen for you. I've never seen him so gone for anyone like he is for you. You're all he can talk about."

I slipped my book into my bag and stood. I wouldn't let Riley sway me. He was Parker's friend. Of course, he'd be on his side.

"I need to go. Don't tell Parker you ran into me. Please." I hefted my pack to my shoulder. "You're a great guy, but I hope I don't see you again. No offense."

157

He lifted his hand. "None taken."

34

PARKER

I STARED AT my friend, wanting to shake him. "No way. You actually saw her yesterday?" Why was he just now telling me? I'd lost sleep looking for Meridee the past five days. Why couldn't I have accidentally stumbled upon her?

Life had a sick sense of humor.

Riley made a face. "She asked me not to tell you, but I thought you should know. But I didn't want you to lose your focus tonight. That's why I didn't tell you earlier." He grinned. "And it worked. You were on fire, man. Nevada has to hate your guts."

If Riley wasn't my best friend, I'd tear his arms from his body. It was still tempting. He'd totally betrayed me. Yes, I had played the best game of my career tonight. Eight receptions for 115 yards and three touchdowns, to end the season with one loss, a bowl game, and a number seven ranking in the AP Poll. Not bad for a small school program that hadn't ranked since 2003. But still. He should've told me about Mare the moment he saw her.

"She was in the Cleveland building?"

He nodded.

"I can't believe you ran into her and conveniently forgot to tell me until now."

"Sorry, man."

I paced in front of the couch. "What floor?"

Riley shook his head. "Don't expect to find her there now. She seemed upset that she had to find another hiding spot."

I pinched my lips. "If you'd texted me right away, I might've found her."

"I don't think so." He gave me a pitying look.

"How did she look?"

"Kind of like you, a bit worse for wear."

I ran my hand through my hair. "This is killing me." I hated that she was hurting, and wanted to fix that.

"What will you do?"

"Whatever it takes." I stared up at the ceiling, my mind churning ideas like fish in an Alaskan fishery. "Maybe I'll use my clout on campus to make her face recognizable. With twenty thousand students walking around and only a week and a half left until finals, I'll need all the help I can get." I rubbed my hands together. "You have a picture of Mare on your phone, don't you?" It killed me that I had absolutely no photos of her. Why hadn't I thought to take any that weekend she'd hung out with me and Mom? Or even a stupid selfie that afternoon we'd driven up into the hills.

Riley pulled out his phone and scrolled. "Here's one of her playing miniature golf on our first date."

I took the phone from him and snorted. Meridee's eyes were half-closed, but oh, the memories that flooded my mind as I studied the photo. I had my arm around Lily's waist, but my focus was on Mare, even then.

"She stunk at putting." I brushed my finger over her face and shared the photo to my phone.

Ry glanced at the picture and chuckled. "I should've realized you liked her that night. You paid way more attention to her than Lily."

Yeah. I had. Why had I wasted so much time with Lily? I had to be the world's biggest fool.

A lump formed in my throat as I stared at her photo. I missed Mare. Big time. We'd just barely made things official between us, but I felt so much closer to her than that. I think my feelings for her had been growing like crazy during the drama of the last few months with Lily. Though Mare was beyond upset and avoiding me to the extreme, I had hoped all during the game that she was watching me, wherever she was. It wasn't like I needed validation, but tonight's performance had been stellar. Everything I'd done had been with the hope of impressing her. Of bringing my girl back. Of fixing what I'd broken.

"She'll hate me for using this," I said. "You caught her mid-blink. Do you have any others?"

He shook his head. "What are you thinking?"

A rough plan had formulated in my mind. "I'm going to plaster her face all over campus." I scrolled through my contacts until I found Ryan Miller's number. He worked for the campus paper and owed me a favor. "I'll get coverage from the local paper. Maybe the news station will pick it up if I build enough hype." When Riley gaped at me, I shrugged. "Might as well use my fame for something I care about, right?"

He pursed his lips. "Meridee won't appreciate being in the spotlight."

No, she wouldn't. But I had to find her. "Then she better come out of hiding, because she soon will be the most well-known face on campus." I sighed. "I love her, man."

Riley slapped my back. "Then let's get moving."

I smiled. "Waldo, watch out. There won't be anywhere my girl can hide once I begin my *Find Meridee* campaign. I'll prove to her and the whole freaking world that she's the only woman for me."

I had to.

35

MERIDEE

*L*UNCH TIME MEANT the student union was packed with people. I found a table near the middle, hoping to blend in with the other students. With my dark brown wig and wire-framed glasses, I didn't attract more than a turned-up nose from most people. For some reason, Parker had started a media campaign to find me a week ago. I'd been forced to wear a disguise or risk detection. Huge *Wanted* posters of me all over campus had sent the student body into a frenzy. Everyone wanted to be the one to present Sticky Fingers with his prize. No matter where I went, I spotted my face plastered on walls or overheard strangers discussing me. So freaking annoying.

Luckily, Aunt Rhonda had a couple of wigs in storage that she'd used during chemo treatments a couple of years ago. Those, along with the nerdy glasses I'd picked up at Walgreens, had made it possible for me to slip into classes and around campus incognito.

Invisibility cloak 1. Parker 0.

He wouldn't win this game.

A full page ad in the *The Daily Evergreen* made me scowl. That horrid picture with my eyes half-closed taunted me from the campus paper. In big bold type, Parker begged his fans to help him find the girl he loved. As if he knew the meaning of that word. If he'd loved me, he wouldn't have wrapped himself up in Lily's arms right after making me feel that I was special. And he certainly wouldn't have plastered such an atrocious picture of me all over campus, making me the laughingstock of the whole student body.

I scarfed down my salad and pulled my calculus book from my bag to review for my upcoming test. When I glanced up to rest my eyes, my fork froze in front of my mouth. Parker Harrington trudged toward me, carrying a tray of food. He looked around and through me, searching for a spot to eat.

A fan called out. "Hey, Sticky Fingers. Any luck finding Meridee?"

I ground my teeth, hating that strangers knew my name.

Thanks a lot, Parker.

"Not yet," he answered. "But keep your eyes open. She has to be around here somewhere."

"Will do, man. We'll find her."

Fat chance. I slouched lower in my seat and raised the paper up to my nose.

Parker grabbed a seat a couple tables away, making me crinkle the edges of the paper. Why did he always choose spots so near? Did he have some type of freaky internal radar?

I observed through long brown bangs as Parker hunched over his burger and kept his head tucked. He normally threw out his winning smile to any and all, gathering friends like a net catching butterflies. But today, his furrowed brow and scowl screamed: *Leave. Me. Alone! Or I'll tear your wings off.*

He turned his face into his shoulder and coughed, then pulled out a tissue to blow his nose. He really did look awful, as Riley had said. He kept his head low, studying his book as he nibbled his sandwich. He didn't look up, even when several giddy girls nearby recognized him and kept pointing and whispering to each other. Usually, he would've smiled, winked, or waved to acknowledge them.

When nothing they did elicited even a glance from him, one of the more perky girls approached. I could tell by his disgruntled expression that he didn't want to be bothered, but he pinched his nose and signed her napkin. When she kept standing there, he buried his face in his book again.

I sort of felt bad for him. It was obvious he wanted to be left alone, but she didn't appear very perceptive. Or she didn't care.

"So, are you and that Meridee girl a couple?" she asked.

His shoulders slumped. "I want us to be."

"She seems familiar, like I might know her."

I scowled at her bald-faced lie.

He glanced up. "Call my friend at the number on the ad. Tell him what you know."

"I could take you there right now. She lives two doors down from me. Super quiet. Sticks to herself."

Parker's eyes narrowed, but I caught a glint of interest. He pushed out his napkin and handed her a Sharpie. "Write your address. I'll have my friend check it out."

She pouted. "If you come with me now, she won't slip away."

Parker's jaw clenched. "I have class soon. Do you want to give me your address or not?"

"Fine." She wrote her apartment number. "Here's my phone number, too. Call me. I can make sure she doesn't escape. And I'll make cookies for you."

I rolled my eyes. This girl was a piece of work.

"Thanks"—he read her information—"Ashlee."

She looked like she might start squealing. "No problem. See you later, Sticky Fingers."

I watched as he hunched lower in his seat and dug into his sandwich between coughing fits.

Then it happened. My worst nightmare.

Bombshell Barbie walked in with two other friends and spotted him. Swaying her hips, she turned guys' heads as she made a beeline for Parker. I balled my hands into fists, quickly repenting of my kind thoughts toward him.

Parker hadn't spotted his dream girl yet. He was too focused on his sandwich.

My blood boiled as I watched Lily point him out to her friends. He'd chosen her over me, which shouldn't have surprised me. Yet it had, because he'd given the impression that he was an honest, decent guy. But he'd totally played me.

Maybe there weren't any heroes left in the world.

Lily grabbed a chair next to him, and Parker began choking on whatever he had in his mouth. He pounded his neck as his face reddened, then threw back a gulp of soda.

I began gathering my things to make a quick escape. I couldn't watch him kiss her again. My dreams already tormented me with that scene a hundred times a night.

"What are you doing here?" He didn't sound happy, which made me freeze with my bag halfway off the table.

I slowly lowered myself back into my seat.

Lily reached up to stroke his jaw. "I'm ready to forgive you for the other night."

Parker yanked her hand off his face. "Seriously, Lily. Do you have rocks for brains? How many times do I need to tell you it's over between us? I tried to say it nicely, but no more. We're through. I've moved on. Haven't you paid attention to the signs all over campus? I'm searching for the girl I love, not the girl who cheated on me."

She dug her finger into his chest. "You're not man enough for me, you spineless—"

My eyes bulged as she called his manhood into question and mocked his virginal status. Totally cruel and uncalled for, even if I didn't like him.

Parker sat there, taking her abuse. Only his red face betrayed emotion. I thought he might defend himself. But he shook his head, picked up his backpack, and stalked away, leaving his half-eaten lunch behind.

I couldn't breathe as I watched him disappear into the gawking crowd.

Riley had told the truth.

Parker hadn't cheated on me.

I blinked, trying to wrap my mind around this new discovery. Parker wasn't a slimeball. Actually, judging by the way he'd restrained his temper in the face of such vile treatment, he was a saint. A hero.

My focus returned to Lily and her friends. A few huge football players joined them at Parker's vacated table. His half-eaten sandwich remained, and I knew he'd be hungry.

The perky blonde next to Lily hugged her. "You're too good for him."

"Yeah." The Thor look-alike wrapped an arm around her. "Fame's gone to his head."

Barbie pushed her gorgeous hair behind her shoulder. "Good riddance. I don't know why I wasted my time on that pathetic excuse for a man." She tickled Thor's chin.

"I told you, baby. The fact that he's besotted over some mouse of a girl who could be Forrest Gump's little sister should tell you he's not right in the head. He can't handle a woman of your caliber."

I clenched my book, wishing to pour my soda over the knucklehead.

Lily huffed. "He met the mouse at Ferdinand's, that cheesy ice cream shop he likes. She had the ugliest hairnet ever and has ghastly freckles. Parker must be losing his vision."

Thor pulled her onto his lap. "But not his virginity."

They both busted out laughing.

Thor nuzzled Barbie's neck. "I have an idea."

That had to be a first, I thought.

"Parker thinks he's so big and bad, but he's forgotten he's nothing without us. I heard if you put water in a gas tank, it ruins the engine. Let's fill up his tank tonight and put that piece of crap truck of his into the junkyard. Help put his priorities straight. You with me?"

Lily stroked his chin. "I always told him he needed a new set of wheels."

I gaped at the jerks and set my paper down. Parker didn't have much money. If they ruined his truck's engine, he'd be devastated. I hurried and made my escape. In my disguise, I didn't even warrant a passing glance from them.

In a quiet alcove in the science building, I sent Parker a warning text.

> *One of your teammates (Thor look-alike) and Lily plan to put water in your gas tank tonight. Overheard them in CUB after you left. Take precautions.*

The churning in my stomach eased somewhat after I hit send, but I still felt awful. I'd totally misjudged Parker and had treated him as the Big Bad Wolf. I recalled his hug with Lily and now could visualize the scene in a whole different light. Barbie had tried to worm her way back into his arms, as I'd suspected, but he hadn't fallen for her tricks. Still, he was a gentleman and wouldn't purposely hurt her. So when she'd hugged him, he'd reciprocated. But he hadn't kissed her or taken her back as I'd imagined. That'd been obvious by his body language and words today.

He'd told her he was trying to find the girl he loved. Me.

I gulped, wondering it that was still true. I wouldn't blame him if he wanted nothing to do with me now. I'd totally let him down. A good girlfriend would've stood by her man, or at least, confronted him and given him a chance to defend himself. And she would've believed what he said, knowing he was the best of guys.

I rubbed my achy head. Parker had tried to tell me the truth. He'd left that voice message on my phone but I hadn't believed him. I'd erased it, letting my vivid imagination and self-doubt make me throw away the best thing that'd ever happened to me.

How could I fix my mistake?

Or was it already too late?

36

PARKER

*M*Y PHONE DINGED with another text. Was it Mare again, taunting me with how she could contact me, but I couldn't call her back? Or was it another text from Riley, informing me of another bogus lead from one of my fans. This *Find Meridee* campaign had turned into a joke. Everyone on campus suddenly knew Meridee, or lived right next door to her, or worked with her, or had seen her in one of their classes. Riley and I had gotten our hopes up too many times to count.

Maybe I should admit defeat. Based off Mare's text a few minutes ago, I'd been sitting close to her in the CUB and hadn't even recognized her. I didn't know how that was possible. Yet, she'd witnessed my ex-friends talking about me just minutes after I'd left. It humiliated me that she'd probably heard Lily's tirade. How had I not seen Mare? I guess if she didn't want to be found, no amount of Waldo-finding publicity would smoke her out. Meridee was a genius, apparently.

I found an empty corner in the Neill Hall and sank onto a couch to check my phone. My eyes bulged when I saw another message from Mare.

I'm sorry.

That's all it said. I scratched my head. Was she sorry my friends had turned on me? Or worse? Maybe she was sorry she'd ever met me. Or...I shuddered. Could this be a cry for help, like Dad had done?

I punched in her number. When I heard her sweet voice say "Hello" on the other end, I bit my quivering lips.

"Thank God, you answered."

"I, uh..."

"Where are you, Mare?" The adrenaline rush had left me weak. My whole body sagged into the stiff cushions of the couch.

"I, uh..."

"I didn't cheat on you. Lily—"

"I know. I'm sorry I doubted you."

I stared at the ceiling, muscles relaxing. "Where are you? I need to see you."

"Um, I..." She sighed. "Abelson Hall."

I threw my textbook in my bag and stood. "I'm on my way. Don't leave."

"Okay."

Three minutes later, I entered the Abelson building out of breath from running the whole way there. I glanced around the main level but didn't see Mare. I pulled out my phone to call her but spotted a petite girl with Mare's unique hair color heading down the stairwell. I jogged after her but got accosted by an eager fan.

"Hey, Sticky Fingers." He grabbed my arm. "How's it going?"

"Fine." I craned my neck to keep from losing Mare as she rounded the bottom of the stairs. I pulled free from his grip. "I have to go. I see my girl."

"Awesome." He turned and yelled, "Sticky Fingers found Meridee!"

Cheers erupted, though I hadn't found her yet, and if she'd heard the moron's announcement, she'd probably run. Mare hated attention.

People clapped and tried to high-five me as I took the stairs two at a time. When I reached the basement level and rounded the corner, I spotted Mare at the far end of the hall.

I sprinted past gaping fans, visualizing Mare as the football I had to catch at all costs. The other students were the defensive team. I weaved around and through them, dodging their blocks as I took another corner too fast, bumping into Mare, who had stopped at a drinking fountain.

I took hold of her arm. "Mare."

She jerked away. "Get your hands off me." The woman I'd assumed to be Meridee smacked my chest.

I stumbled backward. "Sorry. I thought you were someone else." Now that I could see her face, I didn't know how I'd ever mistaken her for my girl. She had to be several years older than most of the student body. Only her hair matched Mare's coloring.

The woman obviously wasn't a football fan, because she didn't appear to recognize me. Tender mercies. She marched away, muttering under her breath about asinine underclassmen.

Someone clapped behind me. I turned to find a strange brunette with thick glasses. Only...as I peered closer, I realized she wasn't unfamiliar.

"Mare?" The dark brown hair and nerdy glasses had thrown me off, but it was her. At least, I thought so.

Her lips quirked in that adorable way I loved, and suddenly I had no doubt.

"Mare!" I closed the distance between us and pulled her into a squeezing hug. No girl had ever fit so perfectly into my arms. "Oh, Mare." I inhaled her vanilla scent. "I've missed you, girl."

She pulled away and nervously straightened her glasses.

That's when I realized we had an audience. A curious crowd surrounded us, watching with rapt attention.

I pulled her closer, ignoring them. "You look like Edna from *The Incredibles*," I whispered near her ear. "Except one hundred times sexier."

She laughed and pulled away, a beautiful blush coloring her cheeks and neck.

"That doesn't look like Meridee," someone said.

"I heard him call her Mare," another voice said.

"Is this the girl you love?" an obnoxious girl asked from the back, jumping up and down to see over the shoulders of those in front of her.

Meridee glanced about with a look of desperation, a look that said *I'm going to run.*

I linked arms so she couldn't escape. "Nope. This isn't Meridee. But I do love this girl." I grinned down at Mare, who acted as if I'd just propped her up in front of a firing squad. "I'd like you all to meet Marilyn, my favorite cousin. She's been living with her family in Qatar for the last five years. I didn't know you'd returned, Mare." I pulled her into a tight hug. "Welcome back, cuz!"

Cheers, claps, whistles, and shouted "Nice to meet ya's" erupted from my fans. Meridee forced a shaky smile as I pushed through the crowd, keeping her close to me.

"My cuz is claustrophobic, so we need to scram. But I'll catch ya'll at the bowl game in January. Keep your eyes open for my Meridee in the meantime, will ya?"

They cheered. A few of the bolder coeds and football fanatics pushed closer to promise they had my back.

"We'll find her, Sticky! Don't lose hope."

"You guys are the best," I said.

I managed to get Mare out of the building and headed to the library.

"Qatar," she mumbled, huffing at our frantic pace. "That was quick thinking."

"I'm full of surprises, cuz." I winked.

She laughed. Music to my soul.

I led her to an empty study room. When the door shut behind us, I took hold of both her arms and grinned.

"Welcome home, sexy cousin."

She shook her head. "This is all your fault."

"My fault you're sexy?"

Her cheeks turned a lovely pink. "No. Your fault I had to wear a disguise."

"I must confess, if you hadn't clapped at my epic failure with that other woman, I might never have given you a second glance. Where are your adorable freckles?"

Her brown eyes crinkled at the corners as she tugged her bottom lip between her teeth. "I have to go. I have a final in fifteen minutes."

"Me, too, actually."

She gave me a sad smile and started to turn, but I grabbed her wrist. "Wait. I just found you. Can we meet later? Have dinner? I'll be done with my last final at five."

"I'll probably be here until six." She made a face. "O-chem."

"Is it at the testing center?"

She nodded.

"I'll wait for you."

"No. Let me go home to my aunt's and change out of my disguise. I'll meet you back here around eight."

"How about I pick you up at your aunt's place?" I wanted more time with her. "There's a freckle," I said, when I rubbed off enough foundation on her cheek.

She pushed my hand away. "Stop. And no. My aunt lives clear out in Colfax."

"Colfax! No wonder I couldn't find you. Remind me never to play hide and seek with you again. You play hardcore." I grinned. "I'm so happy I found you. I really have missed you."

She ducked her head. "Sorry. I thought you—"

I pressed a finger to her tempting lips. "It's okay. I understand. But as punishment for hiding from me, I'm cutting off all blood ties to you. You're no longer my cousin."

She laughed, and the sound filled me with hope.

"I'll pick you up at seven. At your aunt's place. Will that give you enough time to scrape that crap off your face and change back into Mare?"

Her lips twitched. "Maybe."

I handed her my phone. "Type in your address."

She slowly entered her info. "It's thirty minutes away. If that's too far, I can meet—"

"It's not too far. You could be on the other side of the earth, and I'd find a way to be there by seven."

She grinned. So did I.

I'd finally found my girl. All was right with my world now.

37

MERIDEE

*P*ARKER WOULD BE here in ten minutes. Yikes! I shut my car door and raced up to the porch. Why couldn't life play nice? Just once. It seemed to exist to torment me. I bumped into Aunt Rhonda as I flew into the house.

"What happened to you?" she asked.

That didn't bode well. I felt like a disaster, but now I knew I looked like one, too.

"What didn't happen?" I muttered, pushing past her. Everything that could've gone wrong had done so, and in monumental ways. I'd filled up my car after leaving campus, since the needle had rested below empty. But when I'd driven away, I'd remembered the dang gas cap was still on the roof, so I'd pulled over to retrieve it and had noticed my back tire was dangerously low. I'd putted back to the gas station to change it, but the lug nuts had been too tight to turn. And I had strong arms from years of scooping ice cream! I'd had to enlist the help of a burly biker to loosen them, all the while hoping he wouldn't carry me off to be his leather biker babe as payment. When I'd gotten back on the road, I'd hit every freaking red light between campus and Colfax. Even the traffic engineers had it out for me.

"Oh, sweetie." Rhonda followed me downstairs. My grease-streaked hands and face probably worried her.

"Can't talk," I said. "I have a date in ten minutes." With Mr. Universe! I paused to check my phone. "Strike that. I have a date in eight minutes."

She smiled. "Does your date expect a girl with glasses and dark brown hair, or the regular Meridee?"

"He better be okay with either." I didn't have time for a whole makeover.

"Take your time, sweetie. Caleb and I will entertain him until you're ready."

That's what I was afraid of. My moron cousin would probably fart and burp and make a royal fool out of himself for Parker.

"Thanks." I shut my door.

I stripped off my jeans, oil-stained blouse, and sweat-zilla wig, and wrapped a towel around me. I rummaged through my hamper, tossing clothes haphazardly on my bed as I looked for something dressy, but casual.

If only I'd done laundry last night.

The doorbell rang upstairs.

"Crap," I muttered. I wasn't even close to being ready. Of course, Parker would get here five minutes early.

I hurried down the hall to the bathroom to take a quick shower. Minus my hair. I didn't have time to dry it. I scrubbed my hands, but oil had settled into the ridges of skin. Oh well. I'd keep my hands in my lap.

I dried myself off and spritzed my body with cherry blossom spray. I touched up my mascara and added lip gloss, before pulling my hair into a messy top-knot. Totally lazy, but it'd have to do.

Dang flat tire and messed-up light system.

Back in my bedroom, I scowled at my limited outfit options. If Parker didn't already regret liking me, he definitely would after tonight.

I sniffed my favorite pair of jeans. After a vigorous shaking, I pulled them on and grabbed a black t-shirt. Maybe paired with a necklace and cardigan, it'd look sort of dressy.

Yeah, right. And Mr. Rogers looked like Chris Hemsworth if you crossed your eyes just so.

My sweat glands worked overtime. Hyperhidrosis. I'd learned the name my sophomore year. And I was cursed with it. At least, in stressful situations. Yippee. I fanned my armpits. Could anything else go wrong? Not only did I look like a train wreck, but I'd smell like one, too. I hadn't even seen Parker, and my body was spazzing out.

Maybe his friends were right. He was crazy to like me. I was plain and boring. And I was a terrible person for thinking the worst about him when he'd been nothing but kind and good to me.

I should call this date off and go hide my head under a rock. Or a house.

Parker would be better off without me.

38

PARKER

Y STOMACH FELT like pelicans dive-bombed into it as I marched up the cobblestone pathway to Meridee's aunt's house. Spotting her car in the driveway made me know she hadn't given me a bogus address. I'd worried she might. Deep breath in. I faced the door and let it all out. She hadn't seemed angry earlier but she'd still given off a hesitant vibe, making me unsure of our status. I wanted to pledge my allegiance to her heart forevermore. But I still feared she might kick my trash to the curb.

A woman in her thirties opened the door and gave me an open-mouthed, dazed expression.

"I hope I'm at the right place," I said. "Does Meridee live here?"

"You are. Yes, she is. Meridee's my niece." A smile stretched across her face, and I could tell she recognized me.

I stepped into a cozy entryway and held out my hand. "I'm Parker Harrington."

"Yeah." She shook hands. "I know who you are. Meridee didn't tell me *you* were her date. No wonder she's so frazzled. She's running behind."

"I don't mind waiting."

"I'm Rhonda Martin."

"Nice to meet you, Rhonda."

She showed me into a cramped living room, where I took a seat.

"Do you mind if I get my son? Caleb would love to meet you."

"I'd love to meet him, too."

She disappeared and returned with a pre-teen boy in tow. His face lit up when he saw me.

"Sticky Fingers!" he yelled. "Holy shi—" He gargled as his mom's sharp elbow jabbed into his side. He pouted. "I was gonna say holy shindig."

Rhonda rolled her eyes.

I grinned. "You play any football, Caleb?"

"Hey." He yanked his mom's sleeve. "He knows my name." The boy turned to me. "I play flag football every day at recess with my friends. I'm the wide receiver, like you."

"Want to throw the ball out back while we wait for your cousin?" The snow hadn't piled up as deep out here. I could see bits of grass peeking out in the yard.

"You're here for Meridee?"

"Yep."

He made a face. "Why?"

Rhonda pushed him toward the sliding glass door. "Stop hounding him, son." She tucked a football into his arm.

He ran into the backyard. "Ready to see a real player in action?"

His mom sighed. "This one likes to talk smack. Hope he doesn't scare you off."

"I can give as good as he dishes out. Probably better." I tilted my chin. "Want to put some action behind that big mouth of yours, kid?"

"You're on," Caleb said.

We threw the football back and forth, and I gave the kid pointers on form when he wasn't running his mouth.

When Meridee walked out, I jogged over to greet her. She looked amazing, with her real hair up in a messy bun. Tight jeans and a form-fitting t-shirt under a sweater had my mind wandering to places it shouldn't. Yet.

"Nice catch," she said.

"Caleb here has quite an arm. I almost didn't catch it."

"Did you hear that, Dee-dee?" The kid let out a nine-star burp. "I'm gonna be better than Sticky Fingers when I grow up."

Dee-dee? I mouthed, making her roll her eyes.

"You'll never grow up." She tilted her head. "Caleb's one of your biggest fans." She wrinkled her nose. "Run fast and hard."

I raised my hand to fist bump Caleb, making the kid grin.

I winked at Meridee. "Glad you ditched the wig. It kind of freaked me out."

"And the Edna glasses." Caleb chortled.

I laughed. "Ah, we think alike, my man." I reached for Mare's hand, but she tucked her fingers away and foiled my plan.

"Are you two going to kiss?" Caleb asked.

"We will if I have anything to say about it," I said.

The boy gagged as Meridee turned three shades of red.

But I wasn't kidding. I wanted to kiss her bad.

I drove Meridee back to town to eat at the Black Cypress. Riley had suggested it as the best place to romance my girl. We were seated at an intimate table for two, and I had to agree with him. The place had the perfect ambiance to soften and heal a broken heart. At least, that was my hope. I wanted Mare and I to be good again...like we'd been before that cursed hug with Lily that'd sent her running.

I reached across the table for her hand. Time to get everything out into the open between us.

She squirmed and stared at our connected hands. "Parker, maybe we should just..." She chewed her tempting lips. "You and I are so different. This can't possibly work, us together."

She tried to pull her hand away, but I tightened my grip. "I think we can't possibly fail. We're perfect together."

"You said the same thing about Lily."

I grimaced. "I made a mistake. A terrible one. I thought she was perfect...until I got to know who she really was. Then I realized she couldn't be more imperfect for me. But I know you, Mare. Maybe not every single detail. But I know who you are in here." I tapped my heart. "And the more I discover, the more I like you and want to know more. I'm confident that we'll not only work but thrive together."

Her lips puckered, making it difficult to stay on my side of the table.

"But you're one of the most popular guys on campus, even the nation. And I'm...well, I'll always be overlooked." I opened my mouth to protest, but she cut me off. "And I'm okay with that. I'm not saying that to make you feel bad. It's just the truth. I hate attention, and that's all you get."

"I don't like attention, either. It's annoying."

"But you have it. And you can flip the spotlight on anyone else and they'll receive attention, too. Like your stupid campaign to find me. I haven't been able to walk across campus without a wig for over a week."

"Ed-na," I teased.

She huffed. "I'm being serious."

"And you're adorable when you're serious. But that reason doesn't exist in another month. I'm not entering the NFL draft, so after the bowl game in January I'll become just another regular Joe."

Meridee shook her head. "You'll never be a regular Joe no matter what."

"Why? Because I'm really, really, ridiculously good looking?"

She laughed at my *Zoolander* quote. "You think you're being funny, but yes. That's part of it. There are gorgeous model-looking girls who'd give their left hands for your attention."

I scooted my chair closer. "I don't really like left hands." When she scowled, I took her hand. "All joking aside, Mare, no one will give me a second thought when I don't play ball any longer."

"I will."

I squeezed her fingers. "That's why I'll never be able to overlook you. You're probably the only person, besides my mom, who sees the real me."

Our waiter brought out dinner, and we put our conversation on hold. But it wasn't over. It bothered me that she doubted our rightness. I vowed to convince her of my love and about how awesome she truly was. She still seemed unsure. Probably because of what her jerk ex had done to her.

39

MERIDEE

*A*FTER A SCRUMPTIOUS dinner, Parker drove to Riley's place and ushered me inside. Surprisingly, the place was clean. Last time I'd been here, there had been video game equipment and fast food trash all over the floor. Tonight, a huge bouquet of pink roses sat on the kitchen table, filling the apartment with the smell of love. Tension prickled between Parker and I. The kind that made us intensely aware of each other.

"Have a seat," he said, switching on a lamp across the room. "I'll get us something to drink."

Sultry jazz began to play from the other room, making me gulp. I wanted a chance with Parker, yet I feared it even more. I couldn't take another upset, and my imagination had difficulty picturing us working, even if he thought differently. I would ruin everything. My heart seemed to pound in my head as a bead of sweat worked its way down my spine. Where was an industrial-strength fan when I needed one?

Parker returned with a bottle of champagne and two plastic goblets.

"This place is ours for a while." He smiled, making my whole body tingle. "Ry's out with his girl. I thought it'd be quiet and private here, so we could talk...and relax."

He seemed nervous. Welcome to the club. I was ready to puke.

Parker sank into the cushions next to me and wrapped an arm around me. I automatically stiffened, then chided myself for being a baby. I needed to man-up. Or woman-up. Whatever. We'd already gone past this point. So why did it feel like I was back at ground zero? I needed to smile and not shrink from his touch, so he didn't think me a weirdo.

He leaned closer, and my lungs squeezed painfully, even as I screamed at myself not to overthink this. We'd kissed before. It'd been nice. More than nice, actually. But the disconnect in my brain wouldn't repair itself. Muscles became sore from clenching so tight.

Parker frowned. "I won't kiss you, Mare, unless you want me to." He looked down at my lips.

I turned my head. "How can you even like me after what I did? I believed the worst about you. I'm a terrible person." And a freak. I mean, I was having an inner panic attack just thinking about him touching and kissing me, even though I also longed for him to do so.

His thumb caressed my cheek. "We all make mistakes. I made a huge one with Lily. I get why you thought I was cheating on you, but now you know I wasn't. And I hope to prove that I'm not one bit like your scumbag ex. I love you, and I vow before God that I will never cheat on you or disrespect or hurt you in any way. I'll cherish you as you deserve. If you'll let me."

A solitary tear worked its way down my cheek. Parker rubbed it away and smiled. A gentle smile. One that made me finally relax.

Before I could overthink the moment, I leaned in and pressed my lips to his. Heaven help me, I believed him. And I didn't want to live in fear anymore. His arms wrapped around me and I pushed my fingers into his soft hair as we said hello without words.

"Man alive, I've missed you," he murmured between my lips. "You're so beautiful."

I pushed away. "Don't lie." I never wanted a man to lie to me again.

He cradled my face between his large hands. "I'm being straight-up honest. As a church-going Texas boy, I'm not allowed to be anything else." He kissed my nose. "You're the most beautiful woman on the planet to me, not just because of your adorable freckles, your gorgeous brown eyes I can't stop looking into, your soft, silky hair, and your sexy-as-hell body. Though I'm grateful for all those." He waggled his brows, making me bite my lip to keep from smiling.

"I love how you bite your lips, but I'm dying to take over that job for you."

Oh my. He was going to kill me. My whole face burned, but Parker had trapped it between his big hands and I couldn't hide.

"What I love most though is your inner beauty. Your honesty. Your kindness. Your hard-core work ethic. Your dry sense of humor. I love how much you care about others. You're an incredible woman."

I shivered. He was a master at working my emotions just right, pulling the most stirring music from my soul.

He pulled a throw over me, and I wanted to kiss him again. I hadn't said I was cold. I hadn't even realized I was cold until he covered me with the blanket. He seemed to sense what I needed before I did. Which was playing havoc on my heart.

"Want to know what else I love about you?"

"I'm afraid you'll tell me even if I don't." I pulled the blanket up to my chin, basking in its warmth and security.

"I love how smart you are and how determined and strong you can be."

I shook my head. "I'm not strong. Or smart. I'm stupid...and damaged. A nobody."

Parker scowled, and I wondered if this was it. He'd said he knew me, but he didn't. He couldn't. Now, that I'd given him a small helping of my failings, he would leave. Maybe not right this second. But soon. It was inevitable.

"Is that what he called you?"

I swiped the blanket over my cheek as memories pummeled me. The fear. Pain. Humiliation. The despair as I'd watched all my dreams wash down life's drain.

Parker tilted my head. "Talk to me, Mare. Is that what he called you?" He sounded angry, making me cringe. Brody had always been angry with me. I'd never been able to make him happy.

He pulled me close, cradling me into his massive chest. It wasn't passion, but compassion. And that was my undoing.

Years' worth of hurt, anger, and helplessness poured out of me and into him. I'd held it all in, afraid that this would happen if I ever let it out. But like a stuffed closet, now that the door had been opened, everything came tumbling out.

"Let it out, love," he said, making me cry harder.

My whole body shuddered as wracking sobs tore at my ribs and throat. I don't know how long I cried as Parker held me. Long enough for me to dampen his shirt with my tears. Long enough that my eyes stung something awful when my tear ducts finally emptied. Long enough that the pain numbed.

Parker held me for the entire pitiful episode and didn't complain, and I loved him for it. My parents had wanted nothing to do with my story after

I'd returned from my nightmare. Mark had saved me, but he hadn't wanted to hear me hash out my grief, either. He'd felt the best thing for me to do was to forget about it. Move on. Pretend that horrible episode of my life had never happened.

But it had. And those wounds had never healed. They'd festered and cankered inside me, making me fearful, doubtful, and hesitant to give my heart to anyone again.

I sniffed. "I should've boarded the bus for the senior celebration and never left with Brody. I knew that here." I touched my heart. "But stupid, gullible, vain girl that I was, I felt flattered that he wanted to marry me." I groaned. "I was such a fool."

"No. You were sweet and trusting. Good traits. He was the fool."

I shook my head. "He knew exactly what he was doing."

Parker caressed my arms. "Fools always know what they're doing. Did he hurt you?"

"Just when I was bad." I squeezed my eyes shut. I wouldn't cry again. I wouldn't.

40

PARKER

*M*Y BLOOD BOILED as I watched my girl close her eyes in pain. "Bad?" I couldn't believe what she'd just said. What she believed! "Mare, you don't have one bad bone in your body. And even if you did, that wouldn't have given him the right to hurt you." When she still wouldn't look at me, I growled. "Damn him to hell." Actually, hell would be too kind for the loser. How could any guy hurt someone so fragile and sweet? And utterly perfect. But this hidden piece of her life made sense of her skittish nature and the struggle she seemed to have in trusting me, and herself.

She shivered. "I made him mad."

I glared at the ceiling, wishing all sorts of horrible deaths on the jerk who had hurt her. "How long before you left him?"

She bowed her head. "That's just it, I didn't leave him. You said I was strong, but I'm not. I was so ashamed to tell anyone the truth. Mark even called to ask if I was okay, and I told him I was fine. My whole life I'd been raised to be smart and independent. The thought of admitting that I'd screwed up in the worst possible way galled me even more than staying with Brody. At least with him in that cruddy duplex in Vegas, no one knew who I really was. Who I was supposed to be."

She dragged a hand over her face. "I might've stayed indefinitely if Mark hadn't visited unexpectedly and seen my bruises and dragged me away." Her features contorted. "I'm not strong or brave. I let Brody walk all over

182

me, and now I'm damaged. Permanently. I can't trust. I still have night-mares. Believe me, you really don't want to deal with my issues."

I squeezed her hand. "I feel like you're trying to push me away, but I'm not going anywhere. Everyone's a little damaged, don't you know? It's part of being human."

"You're not."

"Wrong." I frowned. "I'm probably more damaged than most." I'd just learned to hide my wounds better.

Her eyes glistened. "Your father?"

The weight of guilt pulled my head down. "Yeah."

"Tell me about him."

Mare's sympathetic gaze made me long to tell her everything. She didn't think she was strong or brave, but she hadn't let the past destroy her. That took strength. She could've wallowed in pity after what her ex had done, but she'd picked herself up and moved on. Maybe that had hindered her healing, or procrastinated it. But she had learned to lift others despite her setbacks. She'd worked hard to achieve her goals. Brody had tried to destroy her, but he hadn't broken her as she believed. She was stronger because of what she had endured and overcome.

"He was a good dad," I finally said. "Took me fishing, camping. Played football with me in the backyard." A lump clogged my throat. Why did it still hurt to talk about him? "Dad was nuts about the game. Coached me from Pee Wee to junior high. But the summer before high school, I met new friends and wanted to play lacrosse with them. He freaked when I told him."

I ran a hand over my head, wishing I had not been so stubborn. "He had big dreams for me, all centered around football, not lacrosse. So when I refused to try out for the football team, he gave me the silent treatment. Refused to come to my lacrosse games. Wouldn't even look at me at the dinner table. It was like I had suddenly become dead to him."

I closed my eyes, still aching inside. "Mom said he'd come around, but I wondered. I hated being ignored. It was worse than him yelling at me. So, I finally caved and talked to Coach about switching back to football, even though it was mid-season. He was totally stoked, and said my starting spot was mine. I came home, excited to tell Dad the good news. I hoped he would talk to me again. That I'd be his favorite, like I had been before."

The horror of that day bludgeoned me, the pain still as fresh and excru-ciating as when I'd been a fourteen-year-old boy. "But I found him..." My body began shaking. This is why I never spoke of him. Why I tried so hard to block it all from my mind. Years had passed, but when I recalled that day, time seemed to reverse and made me relive the horror, agony, and regret all over again.

I took a deep breath, steeling my emotions. "I found him in the garage. He'd turned the car on and asphyxiated on gas fumes."

"Oh, Parker." Meridee squeezed my hand.

I gulped. "I was too late." The image of Dad's limp body slumped over the steering column came unbidden to my mind. I recalled opening the door of his BMW and yelling his name over and over as I tried to move him.

"It wasn't your fault," she said.

I rubbed my temple. "Mom said he killed himself because he'd made bad business decisions and was desperate, but I can't help but wonder if I'd played football, instead of fighting him, maybe he'd be here today. Maybe I would've given him something to live for, you know." I blew out a long breath. "I feel like I killed him."

"Oh, Parker." She pulled me into her arms, and I never wanted her to let go.

"I should've listened to him," I said, choking on the last word.

"I should have listened to my brother. Do you think I got what I deserved with Brody because I didn't?"

"Absolutely not!" I pulled away to look at her. "That jerk took advantage of your innocence. He manipulated and terrorized you. No one deserves that."

"No one deserves the blame for your dad's death either, especially you. You were just a boy exercising free will."

I buried my head in her neck again to hide the emotions breaking through my protective shield. She was right. I knew that in my heart. But it was difficult to believe in my head. She held me like that for a long time, and I savored her love. Her acceptance. Her peace.

I was glad we'd shared our stories. Mom had tried to get me to open up about Dad, but I'd guarded my secret fiercely, never wanting anyone else to know my pain. My regret. Yet oddly, sharing it all with Mare had actually taken some of the sting away. The weight on my chest was gone. I was still sad, and a little angry. But the burden of keeping my emotions locked up tight was gone. And it felt freeing.

"Don't ever leave me." I pulled her onto my lap so my lips could savor hers, so our tongues could caress and play tag, so our bodies could tangle together on the couch. Her hands slipped up my shirt as I kissed her feverishly. Every cell in my body wanted her, yearned for her, ached to make her mine. And by how she held me—clutching me tightly—I could tell she felt the same.

Meridee shuddered beneath me, her lashes fluttering open. The smoldering look in her eyes beckoned me to continue. I wanted to—make no doubt about it—but recalling the disappointment in Mom's eyes years earlier made me groan and roll off her.

"I can't do this." I yanked down my shirt and paced beside the coffee table. I didn't dare sit by her now, as my self-control hung by a thread.

"I overheard Lily call you a virgin," Mare whispered.

I clenched my hands. "She probably thinks I am because I wouldn't cross that line with her. But I'm not." I swallowed. "I got my girlfriend pregnant in high school."

"Oh."

I kept pacing. "Mom was so disappointed. Both of my older sisters had gotten knocked up in high school, and Mom had always pleaded with me to be careful and save sex for marriage." I faced Meridee. "But I screwed up one night and had too much to drink. One thing led to the other. I didn't even like Kalli all that much, but I determined to do right by her when she told me she was pregnant, though that meant giving up my dream of playing football and going to college. I'd seen how my sisters suffered when the guy skipped out on his responsibilities, and no way would I be that guy. So we set a date, and I made plans to support a wife and child."

"So, you've been married, too?"

I dug my fingernails into the palms of my hands. "No. Kalli got an abortion."

Tears glistened in Mare's eyes.

"I hadn't wanted to be a father. I mean, the whole idea of marrying Kalli made me sick to my stomach. But still, when I found out she aborted our child, I was furious." I closed my eyes. "I should've been relieved. I knew I wasn't ready to be an adult yet. But having that choice ripped away from me made being a father the only thing I suddenly wanted. Mom and I mourned for months. I made a solemn vow to her that I'd never compromise a girl again. When I had sex, I'd be ready to be a dad. And my partner would want to be a mom."

"You're a good man."

"But I'm damaged."

She smiled, setting my heart at ease. "I'm glad."

I pulled her to her feet and squeezed her. Then I kissed her again, but this time took it slow. We sampled, savored, and soothed each other, and the cracks in my armor and gouges in my soul filled in with her love. The heavy burden I'd carried for years fell away with Mare's acceptance, and I knew I could face whatever life threw at me, as long as she was by my side.

I caressed her freckled cheek. "I'm not ready to be a dad yet, and I doubt you're ready to be a mom. But you are who I want by my side when that time comes. I've never felt this way about anyone else."

"Even Lily?"

I stuck out my tongue. "Especially her. I kept thinking loyalty to my mom kept me from going all the way with her, but if I'm honest, I knew in here," I pounded my heart, "that Lily would be the worst mom ever. She's too self-absorbed to care about anyone else."

Mare caressed my cheek. "For what it's worth, ever since I saw you play with the kids at the hospital, I knew you'd make an incredible dad someday."

"What about husband?"

She blushed and looked down at her hands. "That, too."

I grabbed both her hands. "You're so adorable."

She shook her head.

I brought her hands to my chest. "Seriously. You're precious to me, Mare. You've made me the happiest man ever. Don't ever doubt that again and run."

She leaned over to nuzzle my cheek.

"Promise me," I said.

Her eyes crinkled at the corners. "I promise."

41

MERIDEE

*M*Y SOUL SHRIVELED like a prune as I entered the stadium. Parker's mom walked beside me, which bolstered my waning confidence. A tiny bit. I held my breath as we worked our way through the energetic crowds. Panic had become my clingy companion in big group settings. I would've been content—even thrilled—to watch Parker's final game on TV, but his coach had insisted on flying his mom and me out to watch the game in person. I guess Pam had really charmed the old softy when they'd met in October.

I tried to think of anything other than the people pressing into me. The past three weeks had been the best of my life. Parker and I had spent every waking second together, besides a few days during Christmas break when I'd flown home to visit my parents. But even then, we'd Skyped several times a day. I found I could talk to him about anything. We'd gotten the hard stuff out into the open, so now, everything else seemed easy.

Campus was mostly empty, and we'd made good use of that after I'd returned to Pullman, making out in several buildings, making out in the gym after Parker worked out, making out in his apartment until Aunt Rhonda texted to get home. Then we'd made out in the parking lot as Parker gave me a long goodbye, acting as though we were parting for years, instead of just until breakfast the next day.

We weren't completely ruled by our raging hormones. We talked, too, and the more I discovered about Parker, the deeper I fell for him. I'd thought he was pretty much perfect before I dated him. Now, I knew he wasn't. Perfect, that is. But honestly, that made him even better. Perfect people are intimidating. And I wasn't frightened or intimidated by Parker any longer. He was my best friend. My confidant. My dream-come-true. I loved him with every fiber of my being. I went to bed with Parker coloring my thoughts and I woke each morning with him at the forefront of my mind. Every second I was awake, Parker was with me, whether we were with each other physically or not. He was with me in my heart. In my mind. My very soul.

Pam located our seats near center field. As I took mine, I started gnawing at a hangnail. Though close to the field, I doubted I'd be able to figure out the plays. Football still baffled me. When the players played, they moved in triple motion so I couldn't keep track of the ball no matter how hard I focused. But then they'd stop and do nothing for stretched-out minutes until the players zoomed all over for thirty seconds again.

Why Parker loved this game I'd never understand.

Pam squeezed my hand. "I know I've said this already, but I can't express how thrilled I am that you and Parker are together. He finally got it right this time."

"You raised an amazing son."

"He's a gem." She grinned. "He missed you while you were with your parents during Christmas. If he wasn't on the phone with you, he was sulking around the house waiting to call you again."

"I missed him, too." I missed him, now. Our flight had gotten in yesterday afternoon, but Parker had been busy with his team, so I'd hardly seen him for the past twenty-four hours. We'd had a couple of hours at lunch today, before he'd left with the rest of the team to drive over to the stadium. Pam and I had passed the remaining time window shopping, before catching a taxi to the game. Parker would take us home after the post-game interview, and we'd visit Disneyland—compliments of his coach —before flying back to Pullman to prepare for next semester.

The cougars played hard, and Parker was on fire. His mom and I cheered and high-fived each other often. By half-time, our team had pulled away by ten points. Parker had made one of the two goals. Or touchdowns. I messed up the lingo constantly.

As the team headed into the tunnels, I glanced up at the Jumbotron right as a busty blond cheerleader grabbed Parker on the field and gave him mouth-to-mouth.

"Oh, dear." Pam shook her head. "What a hoochie."

The camera cut off of them before I could see Parker's reaction. It hadn't been Lily, but still. No girl likes to see her boyfriend kissed by another woman, especially a beautiful one. But my boyfriend—it still felt weird to call him that—was a hot commodity. Girls all across the nation had him pinned up on their walls and dreamed about catching him, just as he caught the football each week. And those girls looked a whole lot prettier than me.

Again, I wondered what Parker saw in me. Would he grow tired of me soon and move on to greener pastures? Was I setting myself up for total heartbreak?

He told me that he loved me, but he'd probably told Lily the same thing, and look what had happened to them. If she couldn't hold his attention—with her flawless beauty—what chance did I have?

Pam began raving again about how perfect I was for her son. She loved to make people feel good about themselves. I nodded politely but could only consider the reasons why I didn't deserve him.

I was nothing special. My claim to fame consisted in having all A's in my major, except for one B+ in organic chemistry—may that subject rot in hell. There wasn't much else I could brag about, besides maybe being an expert ice cream scooper once upon a time.

My stomach tied itself into knots during the third quarter as my gaze drifted to the cheerleaders on the sidelines. They were so beautiful and confident. My polar opposites. Football players and cheerleaders went together like peanut butter and jelly.

I was the *one thing* that didn't belong here.

The fourth quarter started. I tried to focus on the game. I really did. But doubts had me fighting tears. I would never fit into Parker's world, no matter how hard I tried. He couldn't see that now but he'd recognize it eventually. And I'd die when he left me.

I clapped and cheered as he made a second touchdown. Watching him run off the field with a huge grin made me ache. I wished I was prettier, more talented, more deserving of him.

"You're awfully quiet." Pam's hand rested on mine.

I shrugged. "Just thinking."

"Of my son?"

I nodded. "Yeah. He's Mr. Incredible." The perfect hero. Not only was he handsome, but truly kind. He'd been coming by to volunteer at the hospital every week, and the kids, and even older patients, adored him.

"He is."

I chewed my lip.

"You're pretty incredible, too."

"No." I met her concerned gaze and frowned. "I'm nothing special. Not like him."

She wrapped an arm around my shoulders. "Meridee, you are one of the sweetest, most genuine girls I've ever met. My son quite simply adores you because he's finally thrown off his blinders and sees the magnificent woman you are, inside and out. Maybe it's time to take your own blinders off."

I mulled over her words. Ever since Brody, I'd struggled with negative self-talk. Usually, I didn't even realize I was doing it until Mark or a room-mate told me to knock it off. No one liked a Debbie Downer.

"You should ask Park to list the qualities he loves about you." She grinned. "Trust me, the list is a mile long. He kept adding to it the whole time he was home, but you should hear the key points from his own mouth. What I love about you though is your big heart and how you give without expectation. I also love your dry sense of humor. It keeps my son on his toes."

Her words warmed me up like a cup of hot cocoa. No one had ever told me what they liked about me before. My mom and dad told me what to aim for and made it crystal clear when they were disappointed. But they'd never congratulated me for anything I did right. My whole life, I'd chased after their approval. A futile and exhausting quest, I now realized. And probably the reason I felt so tense and uptight around them. I soaked in Pam's kind words, already addicted to them.

"From that first time I met you, I've felt you were a kindred spirit. A friend. I can't say that about many people. Park can't either." She squeezed my hand. "Don't doubt your feminine charms, darling, especially when it comes to my son. I've never seen him so smitten. He loves everything about you, right down to your freckles."

I wrinkled my nose.

She laughed. "It's true. Parker went on and on one night about how adorable your freckles were, and how he couldn't wait to count every single one of them for the rest of his life."

"What a weirdo."

"Yes, but he's weird because he's head-over-heels in love with you, darling."

She pulled away to watch the next play. There were three minutes left in the game, but those three stretched into ten as I ran Pam's words over and over in my head. Actually, I clung to them like frosting on a cake and savored their deliciousness.

Did Parker really talk about me to his mom?

It silenced many of my doubts to know he cared enough to share details of our relationship with her. They were close. That was one of the things I loved about him—how sweet he was with his mother. Maybe a plain ex-ice-cream scooper and a famous football player could get along. We might not be peanut butter and jelly, but we could be peanut butter and chocolate. That was even yummier.

The game ended, and the fans in the stadium went wild. Or wilder. They'd been crazy the whole time. Our team had won by three. Though I knew nothing about football and our opponent, I'd trusted that Parker would lead our team to victory. Whatever he willed came to pass.

Fans began filtering out of the oval chamber of torture, but Pam and I stayed seated. We'd be here for a while, waiting for Parker. I watched the Jumbotron as the newscasters began post-game chatter. They grabbed Jacob, the quarterback, and talked to him about his awesome game. Even Tiny Mo got a few seconds in the spotlight for his impenetrable defense. Lastly, my man's face filled the screen. I tingled at the sight. Even with his brown curls plastered to his head in sweat, Parker looked scrumptious. He panted as he answered the sportscaster's questions, and I admired his poise on camera. I'd be a weeping mess.

The woman wrapped up her interview by saying, "Word of your campaign to find your missing girl in Pullman has spread around the country." A picture of me laughing suddenly filled the ginormous screen.

I froze. Where had they gotten that?

"We heard you succeeded, and that she's here in the stadium tonight."

Parker nodded and grinned from ear to ear as I sank lower in my seat.

"Is there anything you'd like to say to her?"

"Oh, yeah," he panted. "Mare, babe, are you watching this?" He stuck his head closer to the camera and waggled his brows.

Pam squealed and patted my arm. "He's talking to you, darling."

Yeah. That was hard to ignore since his voice carried over the entire stadium and his gorgeous face filled two jumbo-sized screens. I wanted to make like an ostrich and bury my head. But the steel benches of the stadium would hurt.

"I want you to know I love you with all my heart. You're my everything. I don't want to embarrass you on national TV by asking you to marry me but know that's the question I want answered soon. So ponder that, darling."

He blew a kiss and stepped aside as the interviewer retrieved the mic and gushed about how romantic he was.

A few people had spotted me during his monologue, and now pointed and whispered to their friends. Probably discussing how crazy Parker was for liking someone like me.

I cringed as two girls stepped up to our row and waved.

"Yoohoo! Could we take a picture with you, Meridee?"

"M-me?" I stared at them. They had to be kidding.

"Yeah." The one jumped up and down. "I can't believe we found you. And you're so much prettier in person than in your pictures. I want to show my friends that we met Sticky Finger's true love. They'll be so jealous."

Pam walked over as I gaped at them. They thought I was pretty?

"I'm Parker's mom. Let me take your picture with her."

"OMG. I can't believe we're meeting his mom, too. This is so exciting," the other girl gushed.

Pam took a picture of a dazed me standing between the two perky fans. Next, I took a picture with them and her. A few other stragglers who hadn't rushed to be the first to leave the stadium gathered around us. We took more pictures as other fans followed the girls' example. I couldn't fathom why these people wanted pictures with me, but they acted like Pam and I were celebrities. Super weird.

Arms wrapped around me. Thinking a fan was getting frisky, I screamed and jerked around to find Parker laughing. I burrowed my face into his sweaty uniform and closed my eyes.

All this attention was his fault.

"It's Sticky Fingers," someone cried, and the excitement factor went up by three hundred percent.

Parker paid them no heed. He tilted my chin and gazed into my eyes. "Are you okay?"

I nodded. "Good game, but why did you have to bring attention to me during your interview? And where did they get that picture of me?"

He waggled his brows. "I took it the night before you left for Arizona and slipped it to the press. I didn't want them using the mini-golf pic you hate so much, although I think it's cute."

I groaned.

He turned to his fans that were crowding us. "Hey, everyone. Thanks for coming out to support the team today. We appreciate it."

They cheered, and several phones flashed.

"I see you've met my girl, Meridee Mansford." They cheered again. He could've said, "I have a Snickers bar in my pocket" or "I have to go pee" and they'd still have probably cheered.

I maneuvered closer to hide behind his arm.

He kissed the top of my head. "You already know I love her, and I believe she loves me back, right?" He waited for me to answer.

I ducked my head. Where was a good invisibility cloak when you needed one? "You know I do."

"Yeah!" He pumped his fist in the air. "That's what I'm talking about."

He wrapped his arms around me and nuzzled my nose.

I tensed and tried to pull away, because we were surrounded by a claustrophobic crowd and I wasn't a huge fan of PDA.

"Don't they make the cutest couple?" I heard someone say, and several girls sighed.

I glanced up at the big screen over his shoulder and all the air rushed out of me. "Please tell me we're not on live TV." My chest started to squeeze in on itself, but the soft caress of Parker's lips on mine made me close my eyes and ignore the scary world.

"I know this is fast," he murmured between my lips, "but I can't hold back anymore. You remember that talk we had...about sex?"

I buried my head in his neck, hoping no one could overhear him, especially his mom. My skin overheated as I recalled every word of that conversation, and what had transpired before it.

"I remember."

"I want that with you, Mare. I love you and want you to be mine forever. Will you marry me in five more months, after I graduate?" He deepened the kiss, as if he needed to convince me I wanted him. Despite the horrid crowd and media attention, I didn't need any convincing. I already knew I loved him.

"Yes," I answered when he gave me a chance to draw breath.

I felt him grin beneath my mouth, before his hand found mine and drew it up between us. He grabbed a ring his mom held out for him and slipped the diamond solitaire over my finger as the crowd went berserk. I heard clapping, hooting, cheering, and whistling. Someone even rang cowbells. Yeah. Cowbells. But Parker started kissing me as though I possessed the only sustenance left on earth, making it very difficult to focus on the surrounding chaos. Which was good, because I might've freaked if I'd taken a second to realize how we were the center of attention in this massive stadium. Instead, I focused on filling his hunger...and mine. It was impossible to pity myself or give in to doubts when Parker made me feel so treasured.

He was right. We were perfectly matched. He made me complete and whole. Nothing else mattered except our devotion to each other. And we had a lot of that.

We kissed until I leaned back to gaze into his gorgeous blue eyes and touched my new ring. Parker and I hadn't dated long, but I trusted my Nordic god. I trusted Barry Tonanhot, my Huckleberry Heaven, even, dare I say, my Sticky Fingers.

No. I brushed my fingers over his rugged jaw. He could be Sticky Fingers to the world, but to me, he'd always just be my Parker. My heart. The other half of my soul.

"I love you, Mare," he said again, for my ears only.

"I love you, too."

He kissed me again, and the crowd became twice as rowdy, but I didn't mind. I only cared about the man holding me, and truthfully, what we had together was definitely cheer-worthy.

EPILOGUE

$\mathcal{T}$O WRAP UP my love story, let me just say the last semester of school rocked. Mare and I spent every possible second together, and she earned her first C+ in college because of that. She still gives me grief for that, but I feel it's the sweetest C+ she ever earned. In Kissing 101, she earned an A+++. Of course, she had the professor (um, me!) wrapped around her lovely finger.

After I graduated with my bachelor's degree in April, we married in her backyard in Tempe, since she refused to elope. Said her mom might disown her. So would mine. It was the middle of May and one hundred and five freaking degrees outside, but I put up with the hoopla because I kind of had a major crush on the bride. She was adorable in a hot, sexy way that made me want to steal her away and jump straight to the honeymoon.

Our honeymoon was not in Tempe, nor Hawaii, as I wished. Since I'd taken a position with Boeing, our honeymoon consisted of pulling all our belongings in a small trailer behind my truck back to Washington, stopping along the way for honeymoon-like activities whenever the urge hit us. Mare seemed happy, and I was simply thrilled to be with her, so it worked out (although I'm saving to take her some place exotic, preferably with a beach where she'll have to wear a bikini all week).

My new job is great. I'm excited to go into the plant each day and make a difference in the world of avionics. Mare found a job working as a CNA at a hospital near our apartment. She's taking night classes to finish up her pre-med degree and move up in the ranks as she saves for PA school. We spend every spare minute exploring the Pacific Northwest and acting like newlyweds. My favorite way to act. So far, I love Everett, Washington. It never reaches one hundred degrees like in Texas or Arizona, and I'm okay with that.

In truth, I'm fine with whatever as long as Meridee's by my side. If we had to live in hot, dry, parched Arizona or hot, dusty, parched El Paso, I'd still consider myself to be the luckiest man alive. My wife's a wonder. I believed I married the most amazing, kind, talented, and beautiful woman in May, but Mare keeps surprising me. I love her more than I ever imagined possible, and hope she feels the same about me (though don't ask her that at a certain time of month).

The best thing about being married (besides intimacy—because face it, that can't be topped) has been making new traditions. Mare insisted we have dinner together each night, and when kids enter the picture much later down the road, we'll keep the tradition going. She also wants to have a date night each week where we trade off planning the activity.

I insisted on a few traditions of my own, asking that she watch one game a week with me during football season. I'm determined to make a fan of her, although my work's cut out for me since she doesn't know the difference between a field goal and a punt. I also set the first Sunday of every month aside as orange chicken night. She rolled her eyes at that one, but in our eight months of marriage, we haven't missed orange chicken night yet, and she does the cooking, since I suck in the kitchen. I tease her that she should wear the orange chicken, not eat it. After all, that's what made me notice her in the first place. I doubt I would've taken note if she'd been wearing split pea soup or refried beans. But I know for a fact that orange chicken looks delicious on my sweet wife. I definitely wanted to eat her that day in the CUB when I covered her in the sticky meal.

Thankfully, I married my addiction, and can eat all the Mare I want now—covered in orange chicken or not. She's tasty both ways, though I haven't been able to convince her to let me cover her in the sticky sauce again to sample her.

But life isn't over yet. [Insert evil laughter.]

Our life together is just beginning.

ALSO BY CHARISSA STASTNY

Thanks for reading *Game Changer*. If you enjoyed Meridee's and Parker's story, please leave a review on Amazon or another site. You might have to sign into your account first. Reviews help authors and readers by providing helpful feedback. So thanks for your support.

Here are teasers and reviews from my other books, if you haven't checked them out yet. You can find them all on my Amazon page.

Other Ruled Out Romances

Love Notes

Forget about my first kiss? Not when it goes viral.

"Definitely on my top 3 books of the year! I laughed! I totally cried! My heart hurt! My heart smiled. I LOVED this book!" - Amber, reader

Package Deal

Angels come in different packages.

"Once again I went without sleep and got lost in the pages of a fantastic read. The romance was divine, the characters perfect." - Mylissa Demeyer, author

Collateral Hearts

Can a bet lead to love?

"...A heartbreaking and sweet romance all rolled into one!" –Taylor Dean, author

---

Between Hope & the Highway

Can hope bring them together?

"...Perfect blend of plot twists, sizzle, witty dialogue, & even gems of wisdom. I am so in love with this book and I think I will actually read it again—which I never do! (Excepting Jane Austen's of course)." - Amazon reviewer

---

A Wrinkle in Forever

What do you do when forever unravels?

"Be still, my heart...I thought it was going to be a light romance, but it was SO. MUCH. MORE. . If you're looking for a romance with substance, this is it" - LaurenMarieReads, book blogger

BENDING WILLOW TRILOGY

Threads of love, loss, and forgiveness weave an emotional tapestry through this

gripping tale that both inspires and captivates.

Finding Light - 1

Discovering love can be a dark journey.

Guarding Secrets - 2

Time reveals all secrets.

Embracing Mercy - 3

True love must sacrifice.

"A great conclusion to an emotional, fast-paced trilogy. If you like an intense read, lessons in redemption and such, check out this series." - Rebecca Belliston, author

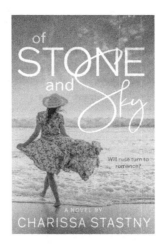

Of Stone and Sky

Can ruse turn to romance?

"Take a chance on this one-of-a-kind romance novel!" - Taylor Dean, author

BOOK QUESTIONS

1. Meridee suffers from poor self-esteem because of what she endured during her first rocky marriage. What signs did you see in her that showed she hadn't quite healed from that trauma?
2. Meridee's parents and family didn't want her to rehash the past after she leaves Brody. How was this 'enforced silence' a setback? Do you think talking about hardships help the healing process? Can it be detrimental?
3. Parker is thrilled when Lily starts paying attention to him. But he soon becomes disillusioned, as is shown in his analogy of his dog Revit and the chocolate cake. Have you, or someone you love, ever wanted something so badly that definitely wasn't right for you/them? What did you do when you figured out you were holding onto the wrong thing or the right thing for the wrong reasons?
4. Parker distances himself from his best friend, Riley, a couple times. First, when Lily encourages him to because Riley isn't cool enough for her crowd. And second, when he realizes he has feelings for Meridee and avoids Riley so he doesn't have to see his friend and Mare together. Have you ever experienced being on either side of this equation—either as the one who distances yourself from others for a good or bad reason, or as the one who is ostracized and doesn't understand why? How can we be more inclusive to expand our circle of friends? How can we be

more empathetic and understanding when we are the one on the outs?

5. Meridee harbors a lot of doubts that hinder her from experiencing complete happiness. Have you, or someone you loved, dealt with those quiet, undermining thoughts, that hinder you from being present and experiencing true joy in the moment? How can we overcome these doubts that block progress and happiness?

6. Parker has held in silent pain and responsibility for his father's death for almost ten years. Suicide affects not only the person who takes their life, but like a rock dropped in a pond, it ripples through a huge circle of family, friends, and acquaintances as well. Have you been affected by suicide's rippling effects? What has helped you heal? Or what has hindered your healing? What lessons have you learned from losing a loved one in this terrible way?

7. What's your favorite flavor of ice cream? Have you ever tried huckleberry (Parker's favorite)?

ACKNOWLEDGMENTS

Successful books don't just magically happen. They have an amazing support staff behind them. Mine includes: Susie Poole, my fantastic cover artist; Jenny Proctor and Emily Poole, my eagle-eye editors; and beta readers who provide invaluable feedback before my books are published. I thank them all for their skills and talents. I'm grateful that my husband and children allow me time to write, revise, and edit at all hours of the day and night. They are my biggest inspiration for writing happily-ever-afters...because they are mine. Last of all, thank YOU for taking a chance on my book by reading it.

ABOUT THE AUTHOR

CHARISSA STASTNY is an avid reader, happy writer, and lover of irises, clouds, chocolate, sushi, and the great outdoors. Though she was born and raised in Las Vegas, Nevada, she has never pulled a handle of a slot machine and can't shuffle cards to save her life. She's lived in Nevada, Idaho, and currently resides in central Utah with her husband, four children and their families, where shuffling cards isn't required. She has authored ten books and hopes to *imagine-eer* many more.

Made in the USA
Coppell, TX
18 December 2022

89996460R00118